Borrowed Money

Copyright © 2008 Jim Ardoin
All rights reserved.
ISBN: 1-4196-2046-0
ISBN-13: 978-1419620461
Library of Congress Control Number: 2005910429

Borrowed Money

Jim Ardoin

2008

Borrowed Money

CHAPTER 1

In the still darkness of the master bedroom suite Megan Cedars moaned softly in response to Peter Ferrell's delicate touch. Her steady partner knew precisely what she liked and focused on satisfying all of her deepest needs and desires. "Ooh don't stop," she pleaded. "Aah, that's the spot!" The couple had not been intimate for several weeks and she craved the narrowly focused attention she was receiving. Her long sculptured body stretched endlessly across the cool rumpled bed covers as Peter explored every square inch of her smooth supple flesh.

"Do you like this?" he asked as he traced small concentric circles on her quivering stomach. His slender fingers rarely touched her taught skin, as he allowed them to gently float at that narrow boundary of extreme sensitivity. The uninhibited excitement, free flowing in the electrically charged atmosphere of the small bedroom was palpable.

"You know I do," she purred as her face turned flush red with pleasure. "That's the only reason why I come over here." Megan twisted in delight as she uncrossed her legs to allow her lover unfettered freedom to explore the most sensitive areas of her anatomy. About a year previous, Megan opted to try a full Brazilian. After the initial shock, she found that the complete absence of pubic hair greatly enhanced every nuance of sexual pleasure. She delighted in Peter's reaction when she removed her petite thong and revealed her childlike baldness for the first time. For the longest, he found it impossible to resist touching and stroking her silky smoothness. She responded by relishing every sensual moment. "You do all the naughty things that turn me on so completely."

The couple's erotic activities were suddenly shattered by the unwelcome sound of the telephone ringing on the night table adjacent to the bed. Peter's attention was instantly redirected away from Megan.

She groaned loudly in disgust as he instinctively moved in the direction of the sound.

Peter tried in vain to look around the room, but absolute darkness shrouded all. "Who is calling at this late hour?" he cried in response to the racket. In one quick move, he slid to the side of the bed nearest the phone.

Megan reached out to restrain Peter, but he moved out of her reach. She sat upright and pleaded for him to return to her side. "Let the damn thing ring Sweetie. We haven't been together for a few days and I really need you right now." She slid near him, extended her arms and wrapped them gently around his muscular torso.

The soulful pleadings of his companion went unanswered as Peter pried himself from her delicate embrace. "They're probably calling from the terminal. There's a problem they can't handle."

"Who is going to handle my problem?" she asked tritely as she fell back onto the bed. "Why do you have to deal with every two bit crisis at that fucking terminal?"

Peter ignored Megan's pleadings once again. At the edge of the bed, he draped his legs over the side and reached for the lamp. Under the lampshade, he found the switch and after a quick twist, a soft yellow light bathed the area around the night table. He sighed heavily and reached for the phone. "Ferrell speaking."

The caller barked out his greeting in a quick business like rhythm. "Peter, this is Jeff Deutsch from Union Bank. Did I wake you?"

"No. I'm still up," Peter confessed as he reached across the top of the night table and picked up his alarm clock. The bright red digital dial displayed the time, two minutes before midnight. He quickly racked his brain but was unable to think of a single reason for his banker to call him at home regardless of the time.

"Let me apologize in advance for the late hour for my call," Deutsch offered. "I trust that I'm not disturbing anything."

"What do you want?" Peter responded in a brusque tone. "What on earth can't wait until tomorrow?" Peter demanded as he returned the small alarm clock to the night table. With no response coming through the phone, Peter continued to admonish his banker. "It's damn near midnight. Where the hell are you calling from anyway? You can't possibly be at the office at this ungodly hour."

"I'm not at the office. I'm at home," the caller acknowledged. "I know I should have called you earlier, but I wasn't sure it was the right thing to do under the circumstances," Deutsch confessed. "Maybe I shouldn't have called at all," he continued suggesting he was about to end the call. "It's probably better if I come out to the terminal tomorrow so we can discuss the matter when you are rested. Just forget I called," Peter's banker offered in an apologetic tone.

"It is fine Jeff," Peter insisted as he ran his fingers through his hair to brush it from his face. "You've called, so let's discuss whatever is on your mind. It must be serious or else you wouldn't have called."

Deutsch hesitated for a moment. A little time was what he desperately needed, a few seconds at most, to mentally rehearse the lines of his prepared script. After a quick shallow breath he repeated the words under his breath one last time before disclosing to his client the reason for his urgent call. "Since I have been at the bank, what is it, almost a year now; you and I have discussed this matter I know several times. Unfortunately, I don't think you ever took my warnings seriously."

"What warnings?" Peter demanded growing tired of Deutsch's inability to get to the point. "I clearly remember you have whined often and loudly that the interest rate on my company loan was too low. You have also bitched incessantly that I didn't keep enough money in my checking account, but I don't remember anything serious, certainly nothing that merits a midnight call. So get to the fucking point of your call," Peter ordered his patience at its end. "Drop the cloak and dagger routine." He was already growing tired of the call and he was more than willing to let Deutsch know exactly how he felt.

Peter's swift reaction and his challenging tone surprised Deutsch. He was expecting Peter to remain silent so that he could complete what he had to say without interruption. With his weak poker hand called, he moved quickly into the main body of his script, directly into the reason for the phone call. "The bank has been concerned about the viability of your business for several years. Our files on your company are well documented regarding numerous meetings with you detailing the bank's concerns. These discussions date back well before my arrival here at Union Bank. With the recent rise in diesel prices, the execs at the bank are worried that you may be forced into a chapter proceeding. In a liquidation scenario, the bank stands to lose a considerable chunk of its investment."

The banker's hard-hitting comments caught Peter by surprise. Whatever cobwebs clouded his thinking were immediately brushed aside. "Liquidation!" Peter roared into the phone. "There are no plans to voluntarily liquidate my company."

Peter's quick reaction was exactly what Deutsch expected. Without a second's delay, he went on the defensive. "I'm not talking about a voluntary liquidation. Our fear is that you will be forced into an involuntary bankruptcy proceeding," Deutsch stressed trying his best to maintain control over the conversation. "Transportation Management Services is a great company; however, we believe high fuel prices will absorb all of your free cash over the next few months and you will quickly be forced into a position where you cannot keep your trade vendors paid current. Once in bankruptcy, working capital financing will be unavailable and the fleet will be parked, and we believe permanently. When wheels aren't turning, cash isn't coming in. It's simple math."

Peter stood then started to pace back and forth on the narrow strip of carpet parallel to the bed. As he did the long coiled cord to the phone bounced wildly. His voice rose with each step as he responded to his banker's assertions. "This is one hell of a time to discuss your bank's concerns about my company's financial condition. I have repeatedly told you as well as your predecessors that the business is well positioned and well capitalized to survive anything that comes our way. Our current cash reserve at TMS is more than adequate to offset the negative effects of a spike in fuel prices. Most of our contracts contain provisions to address increases in fuel. Over the past several years fuel prices have fluctuated wildly and we have suffered no adverse effects. The recent rise in the price of fuel is simply a nuisance we can easily manage just as we have in the past." With his voice raised even further, Peter continued in obvious frustration. "What do you expect me to do at this hour?"

He removed the phone from his ear, leaned forward slightly and placed it on his thigh. After several deep breaths, he swore under his breath with sufficient loudness that his caller could hear every word. "Fucking bankers!" He inhaled deeply several times then returned the phone to his ear. "I can bring you all the latest numbers first thing in the morning. Woody and I will walk you through the results from last quarter. You will see that the company is beating budget estimates and that we are not teetering on the brink of bankruptcy as you fear."

At first Deutsch appeared to stumble in crafting his response. He paused momentarily and took several deep breaths. Finally, he was emphatic with his customer. "That won't be necessary."

Peter sat on the edge of the bed. Through the phone he clearly heard Deutsch sigh deeply. It seemed to Peter that his banker's voice was on the verge of cracking, but Deutsch continued undaunted in a staccato like rhythm. "Earlier today the bank sold your loan to an investor. The matter is out of my hands. My call tonight is merely a courtesy. After working with you over the past year, I thought I owed you more than the obligatory form letter."

With the bad news delivered, Deutsch fell silent. He said nothing for at least thirty seconds. He waited patiently for Peter to take the lead and acknowledge his acceptance of the finality of his situation. Peter remained silent, refusing to speak to his banker. Deutsch waited then decided to probe for a reaction. "Peter?" he started in a more subdued tone, "do you understand what I just said?"

"I heard you clearly," Peter responded his mind quickly disengaging from the call. "The bank is concerned about our financial results. It's late so I think it best that we meet tomorrow and straighten this out. Woody and I will come down to the bank when it opens in the morning."

Deutsch shot back. He needed closure and certainly did not want to agree to an early morning meeting. "That won't be necessary.

You have not heard a single word that I have said. The bank no longer owns your loan. It was sold earlier today. There is nothing further for us to discuss"

"What!" Peter screamed immediately returning to the conversation. "Say that again! What did you sell?"

The abrupt change in the tone in the conversation caused Megan to move near Peter at the edge of the bed. She placed her hand ever so softly on the side of Peter's head and gently pulled him near. The electricity in her touch startled Peter. He attempted to pull away but she held firm. She whispered softly into his ear. "What's going on?"

Peter didn't bother to cover the phone. He intentionally spoke in a normal voice so that Deutsch could clearly hear his every word. "It's Jeff Deutsch from the bank," he said in acrid tone. "He says that Union Bank sold the company. It seems our numbers don't meet the bank's expectations."

"They can't sell the company," Megan replied tersely. "There must be some mistake."

"Calm down Peter. Everything is fine," Deutsch interjected upon hearing the discussion between Peter and Megan. "We didn't sell your company, only your loan. You will no longer make loan payments to bank. Instead, you will make payments to the new party."

"I have a deal with your bank, not another party!" Peter yelled into the phone. "I'll sue Union Bank and that includes you personally, you bastard!"

The conversation between Peter and Jeff had deteriorated to a shouting match. Before it reached the point of no return, Megan decided to intercede in an attempt to salvage the company's relationship with Union Bank. She placed her hand on Peter's shoulder to get his attention. "Let me talk to him," Megan suggested. "I'll get to the bottom of this."

Peter handed the phone to his girlfriend then moved to the center of the bed.

Megan slid to the edge of the bed and stood. "Hello Jeff, this is Megan Cedars. What in heaven's name is going on? Peter says the bank sold the company. That's impossible since you don't own the company."

As she spoke into the phone, she opened the top drawer of the night table and searched for a notepad. Tucked away in the corner of the drawer she found a small notepad and pencil bearing the name of The Venetian Hotel and Resort in Las Vegas where she and Peter vacationed earlier in the year. She placed the pad on the top of the night table and prepared to jot down whatever salient points Deutsch provided.

"That is correct Megan," Deutsch said calmly. "We didn't sell the company. The bank merely sold the note to a third party investor. The closing was consummated earlier today in the office of the bank's general counsel. We sent the formal notice to TMS' offices by messenger service immediately after the papers were signed. I expect that they will be on Peter's desk when he arrives at the terminal in the morning."

"So you are telling me this is a done deal."

"Money has been exchanged."

"Who is the buyer of our note?" she asked in her normal reserved tone. "Are you at liberty to disclose that information?"

"Venture Funding, LLC."

Megan adjusted her grip on the phone so she could write the purchaser's name on the pad. "I've never heard of Venture Funding. Do they have a presence in the local market?" she asked as she placed a large question mark after the purchaser's name. She held up the notepad for Peter to read. He grasped her arm and pulled to notepad closer. At first he couldn't read the name clearly since he was some distance from the lamp. He sat up and leaned into the light. After seeing the name, he moved his head from side to side, indicating that he too did not recognize the name of the company. "I don't think we are familiar with this outfit."

"I'm certain you know of them," Deutsch said confidently. "It is based out of Chicago and is quite well known as a major player in the secondary market for bank paper. You have no doubt heard of Venture Funding's owner Marler McAdams."

Immediately Megan recognized the owner's name and responded to Deutsch nearly shouting into the phone. "Marler McAdams! You sold our promissory note to Marler McAdams! Why he's a worthless crook."

Peter sprang from the bed, pulled the phone away from Megan and demanded, "Let me talk to him!" He leaned against the night table and screamed into the phone berating Deutsch. "Are you telling me that you sold our business to that SOB Marler McAdams? He has a reputation as a world-class bottom fisher. The only reason he will buy into a deal it to split up the company and sell its valuable parts. The only thing left behind in his wake is a trail of wreckage."

Megan knew all to well Peter's quick temper and placed her hand on his chest in an attempt to calm him. Her efforts were futile as Peter's rage surged. She tried to retrieve the phone, but Peter would not release it from his crushing grip. Each time she attempted to touch the phone, he turned and moved it out of her reach. In frustration, she again sat on the edge of the bed.

"Listen to me Jeff! Woody and I will be at your desk in a few hours and we can get this matter resolved." With nothing remaining to say to his banker, Peter slammed the phone onto the receiver.

Megan sensed that Peter was about to lose control over his emotions. She knew far too well of his explosive temper and from all indications it was ready to erupt violently. She eased herself off the bed and moved behind him placing her slender arms around his chest. Standing on the tips of her toes, she whispered softly into his ear, "I know you are angry. So am I but absolutely nothing can be accomplished at this hour. Don't let your temper completely control your thinking. Please can we pick up where we were before that awful phone call? I wasn't finished and I know you certainly weren't."

Still Peter wouldn't budge. He remained as rigid as a stone statue breathing more deeply with every heavy breath. Megan's solicitations when unnoticed.

Not willing to give up without a fight, Megan moved her hands lower on Peter's abdomen. She was confident that a little focused attention would certainly help change his nasty disposition. After some tender caressing, she cooed, "Let me make everything better."

Still Peter did not respond. Megan could not remember a time previous when he was so angry. She again tried to calm him. "Tomorrow at the office I will pull my copies of the loan documents, review them along with the security filings so I can determine an appropriate response to the bank's action. I am fully confident that we can waltz into the county courthouse later in the week and get the loan sale nullified, or at a minimum prevent McAdams from taking any action until we have time to gather all of our forces. The bank's actions in this case are indefensible under any legal interpretation."

Peter was not listening to Megan's reassuring comments. His mind was spinning and his thoughts were blurred by his building rage. He broke free from Megan's bear hug and began to pace back and forth on the side of the bed.

Megan tried one last time to snap Peter out of his fit by patting her hand on the bed. "Come here and…"

"I have to do something about this," Peter insisted as he returned to the night table. He picked up the phone and hit the speed dial. Within a few seconds, Megan heard someone answer but she did not immediately recognize the voice on the other end of the phone.

"Woody," Peter nearly shouted. "I need you to pull together the latest numbers for a meeting at the bank first thing in the morning. Go into the office early if necessary. Also, start making calls to other banks. See if we can move our relationship away from Union Bank immediately. You're my chief financial officer. Use every marker you have in this town and call in every favor." While Peter barked his orders to his subordinate, he observed that Megan walked out of the room. "Where are you going?" he called. Megan did not react to his question nor did she reply.

He quickly completed his business with Woody, hung up the phone then followed Megan into an adjoining bedroom. The only light source entering the room came from a streetlight outside one of the large shuttered windows. Among the shadows, Peter found his statuesque companion dressing. "What are you doing?" he asked as if nothing was wrong. "I think we have some unfinished business," he whispered slyly.

"I'm going home," Megan barked curtly. "I came here tonight to grab a little romance, but it looks like I'm just going to get fucked!"

She finished buttoning her blouse, grabbed her purse from the bed and shoved her bra inside.

That was the last straw. Peter's temper exploded into a full-blown rage. "I'm sorry!" he screamed. "My company is going down the crapper and all you want to do is get laid!"

Megan turned and glared at Peter without responding to his vulgar comment. Without being told Peter instinctively understood that he stepped deeply into a rancid pile from which he would be unable to easily recover. His ill-chosen words could not be retrieved and their flagrant use ruined any possibility of immediate reconciliation. At first, Megan did not react overtly to Peter's remarks. She appeared restrained, too restrained for Peter.

She pulled her car keys from her purse and paused momentarily. Her legal training kicked in as she chose her words ever so carefully. "This affects both of us, not just you. I too am mad as hell but there isn't a goddamn damn thing I can do at this instant." She brushed past Peter on her way to the door. "Get out of my way."

Peter pulled his temper back a notch and addressed Megan. "I'm fucking sorry."

Megan stopped dead in her tracks. He immediately knew that he had screwed-up again by not keeping his mouth shut. His ill-chosen words were about to come back to bite him in the butt. With his thoughts controlled by his rage, a lowly I'm sorry was the best he could muster.

Megan threw her purse and car keys onto a nearby chair and pulled the trigger on both barrels. There was no cover for Peter to hide. He stood naked, totally unprotected from her impending verbal assault. She leaned in closely. "That's your answer for everything. You're a fucking hothead and frankly I've had enough. I have to tolerate your infantile behavior as your lawyer, but I'm not going to take it anymore as your bitch."

Peter moved back a half step from Megan and said, "This action by those bastards at Union Bank is unconscionable. I am at a loss as to why they would do this to us after all we have done for them. I never thought anything like this could happen to me."

After taking a deep breath, Megan shot back immediately. "I told you four years ago to move your loan away from that fucking bank. I could see then that they were not serving your needs. TMS was nothing more than a house account that they believed was in their pocket permanently. You have been treated like a doormat for years"

"Don't you think that advice is a little late considering what just happened?"

"That's why you should have moved your relationship to another bank four years ago. It was the best thing you could have done for your company. You sit in the chief executive's office, when are you going to start acting like a chief executive officer?"

"I did then and I am doing now what I think is best for my company. That's when we..."

Megan held out her hand to stop Peter from saying another word. "We both know why you didn't move the loan. It's because your daddy banked at Union Bank. And heaven forbids you might change anything your precious daddy did." Before Peter could respond, Megan finished unloading the magazine on her verbal assault. "The only fucking thing your daddy did a world class job on was his marriage to Valerie. He did a world-class job totally fucking that up! I have never seen any individual so unhappy as Valerie Ferrell!"

Megan grabbed her purse and car keys from the chair and moved toward the door. Before she exited, she turned to admonish Peter one last time. "That's your problem," Megan blurted out. "You attack every problem head-on. Kick 'em in the balls and see what they do. That's your strategy. You never think first. Hell, you never think last. Maybe the bank is right and a relationship with you is not in their best interest, maybe it never was. Okay, I agree that selling to Venture Funding was pretty damn shitty under any circumstances. Maybe we will have to get down and dirty, and scratch some eyes out before the curtain falls on the last act. At this moment I don't know what should be our first move. Unlike you I need facts, plenty of facts before I launch the missiles at my opponent. I'm leaving. I have a heck of a lot of work to do to stop this runaway train from barreling over your sorry ass."

"I do what works!" Peter screamed. "And I've been pretty damn successful at it"

"Your tactics may work fine when dealing with union organizers and dumb-ass truck drivers. Now, you're swimming in a shallow pool chocked full of sophisticated sharks with razor sharp teeth. They are going to tear you to ribbons if you don't use a truckload of finesse," Megan screamed in an acrid tone. "Truckloads! Now that's something even your pea brain can understand."

Her biting comments immediately softened Peter's disposition. He reached out to grab Megan's arm in an attempt to reconcile, but she was gone. She rushed out of the room and walked swiftly down the hall to a door leading into the garage. "I'll call you on your cell when I know something." Without another word, she was out the house. The door closed with a loud thud that reverberated throughout the small house.

Peter heard the tires on her BMW convertible squeal as she pulled away from his house. He didn't go after her. Sure he was upset with Megan, but just maybe there was some truth to her to her statements. He was reserving the bulk of his anger for his banker, the man he would face within a few short hours. After so many years of a perfect banking relationship, Peter could not accept that Union Bank, his steadfast financial partner through good time and bad so cavalierly pulled the rug out from under him without so much as a trite apology. From Peter's perspective, this situation looked like a mile of multicolored yarn tied in a million knots. This unfortunate turn of events would not be resolved easily. At a minimum, it would require him to dig deep into his knapsack and skillfully play every trick he found.

Upon his return to the master bedroom Peter retrieved his robe from the bed and left the bedroom. The evening's activities were complete.

CHAPTER 2

Peter entered the breakfast nook in his house and glanced at the large ornate grandfather clock standing guard duty in the corner. As he turned into the den, the clock sprang to life sounding its familiar chorus announcing the time, one o'clock in the morning. Peter realized that it was exactly an hour since his conversation with Jeff Deutsch, a conversation that in an instant changed his life. The potential impact of the bank's untimely action could not be underestimated. The implications were unknown but regardless were certainly critical. Immediate action was the order of the day. Unfortunately, clear thinking was proving difficult to muster at this early hour.

The more Peter thought about the bank's actions the more his level of anxiety subsided. Maybe there was nothing to be seriously concerned about with this sale. It was after all quite possible that Marler McAdams' intentions were benign and Peter was overreacting. If he could determine why Venture Funding purchased the note, maybe he could plot a plausible strategy to make the best of his current circumstances. As far as upside for the new owner, the company's loan was current and the interest rate was bound by contract. Venture Funding was locked into the bank's deal until the scheduled maturity date, which would not occur for five more years. What possible upside did McAdams see in owning the company's loan? The numbers didn't add up. No matter how many times Peter ran the numbers, he kept rolling snake eyes.

As he sat in the cool darkness of his den, Peter anguished over these questions. Soon, he realized that he was over-thinking the problem. Megan would find a quick solution to their predicament before lunch. She was one damn fine attorney and never let him down before. He reached for the remote and turned on a large plasma screen television, which hung from the far wall of the room. Without looking at the buttons on the remote, he quickly tapped the channel numbers for CNN. With his feet resting comfortably on an over-stuffed ottoman, he eased his head into the deep cushioned pillow back of the recliner. It was late and he was tired. As he racked his brain for answers, he slowly drifted in a sound sleep.

Peter's slumber was shattered by a loud sound coming from the street side of the house. He sprang from the chair and with the morning sun cascading into the room through the plantation shutters he turned and again looked toward the clock. To his surprised it was five thirty. He managed to grab over four hours of much needed rest. As he stood to investigate the noise, he flicked off the television. At the front of the house, Peter peered out only to find the city's garbage crew collecting refuse sitting along the curb.

He slowly returned to the kitchen. Once there flipped the switch on a small coffee maker and within a few minutes poured a large mug of black coffee in to his favorite mug. His coffee brand was Community, a stout Cajun blend. He cultivated a taste for this regional coffee during summer visits with his maternal grandmother in south Louisiana.

With coffee mug in hand, Peter moved to the dining table where he filled a small bowl to nearly overflowing with corn flakes. When both the bowl and the mug were empty, he placed them in the sink for the house cleaner to wash later in the day. The coffee had the desired effect. The spark of life was now coursing through his body and mind as the large shot caffeine brushed the cobwebs from his consciousness. He started to think clearly. Megan was right, there was an easy solution to this quandary and if he played his cards selectively, business as usual would return in only a few days. Before all of the acts of this play were complete, the sale of the loan may well turn out to be a blessing. If there was a silver lining in this dark cloud, Peter hoped it materialized sooner rather than later. He returned to the master bedroom and within a half hour, was showered, shaved and ready to start the day.

A warm muggy Houston breeze greeted Peter as he opened the door to leave. He grabbed his cell phone from the edge of the counter and clipped it to his belt. Instantly, he observed that Megan failed to close the garage door when she left in a huff. Peter climbed into the cab of his black four-door Ford F-250 pick-up truck, fired up the massive diesel then backed into the street. Within three blocks he was traveling west on Bellaire Boulevard, heading toward Loop 610.

The massive tires on the imposing vehicle squealed as Peter, impatient to get to the office, forced his reluctant pick-up onto the northbound ramp feeding traffic onto the Loop. Peter pushed accelerator almost to the floor, checked for an open lane then rapidly merged into the brisk flow of morning traffic. An enormous cloud of black smoke billowed from the truck's huge exhaust pipe.

Peter judged the traffic level to be normal for a weekday morning. He knew that when it comes to traffic, the City of Houston was world class. Its freeways were always humming, choked full of speeding vehicles of all shapes and sizes. To the locals, speed limits were merely suggestions to be completely ignored. Out-of-towners were easily identified in the maze. They drove hesitantly and always appeared completely out of sync with the orderly flow of the chaos. The most feared vehicles occupying large expanses of valuable paved real estate were large 18-wheelers that neither stopped nor slowed for anyone or anything. When they went awry, only small pieces remained to be swept from the heavily scarred surface of the roadway.

For his daily trek to work, Peter traveled for almost fifteen miles on Loop 610. The most dangerous section of the Loop consisted of a four-mile stretch that passed through the exclusive Post Oak area of town. This section of freeway was affectionately known to the locals as the West Loop. Sitting squarely in the middle of this massive office center was the world famous shopping emporium called The Galleria. Almost every weekend, Peter and Megan shopped and dined in the vicinity of The Galleria

This day, Peter wasn't concerned about the traffic. As he passed the Post Oak Boulevard exit, he looked to his left and stared for a few seconds at Four Leaf Towers, a high rise condominium development where Megan lived. The only matter controlling his hurried thought processes this bright morning was returning normalcy to his life, especially his love life. The morning sun reflected brightly off the thousands of glass windows encasing the many tall buildings rising within only a few yards off the pavement. It was a picture perfect day and without any delays, he should be in his office within forty minutes.

When he started the business nearly fifty years earlier, Dewey Ferrell, Peter's grandfather selected a location for the company's terminal on Breen Road on the far north side of Houston. After his death, Peter's father John repeatedly drew up plans to move the office to the southwest side of the city. Since the demands at the terminal consumed his every waking minute, a move never materialized. Upon his graduation from the University of Texas ten years earlier, Peter bought a home in Bellaire, a bedroom community on the west side of Houston, and took his place in the management of TMS. Many of his college friends also bought in the area and Peter never thought he would make the drive for too many years. He was confident his father would move the office to a location only a few miles from his home. Once again a move never materialized and over the period of his residency, Peter grew to thoroughly enjoy living in Bellaire.

At the time Peter originally purchased the fifty-year old house his plans were to demolish the structure and replace it with a large modern structure. Over the years however, he grew fond of the old house and sunk considerable funds updating the interior. Once he thought about selling and moving to either Kingwood or Atascocita. These were high-end developments with large expensive homes well suited for well-heeled business owners, highflying corporate executives and high paid lawyers. Both developments would offer a significantly shorter daily commute. Before he could seriously begin a search for a new house, he was forced to take over the business when his father died unexpectedly. In the early years of his stewardship of the company, Peter planned a move of the business and like with his father, the hectic work schedule soon forced him to place the all of his plans, both personal and business, on the back burner.

Exactly at seven fifteen, Peter maneuvered his truck into the parking lot at Transportation Management Services, a regional truck terminal providing both long-haul and regional freight services. The operation at the terminal ran continuously twenty-four seven. The morning hours were the most hectic and on this morning the facility was steaming along at maximum capacity. Over-the-road tractors with the letters TMS stenciled in bright red paint on their doors were in the queue to hook up trailers for delivery across the country. It was a model of efficiency. Peter's grandfather knew the business and Peter's father held a master's degree in transportation engineering. Between the two of them they designed and built an incredibly efficient facility, which although small by industry standards, could efficiently compete with the largest long-haul carriers. The company enjoyed a loyal well-trained team of managers, office staff and operators. Combined with a stellar reputation in the industry, profits were consistent and serious problems were non-existent.

After the death of Peter's father, many customers and competitors alike questioned whether Peter could fill his shoes. No one questioned that he knew the business having worked at the terminal since he was a teenager. Although he carried in his back pocket a business degree from The University of Texas, his employees were unsure whether he had either the total commitment or mental horsepower necessary to make the business a continued success.

Peter fully understood that it was difficult if not impossible to fall head over heals in love with a company build by others. Since taking over the reins at TMS, he had assembled a record of hard work that he believed was beyond reproach. On many occasions he acknowledged openly to his friends that he did not share the same absolute passion for the business as his father and grandfather. Nonetheless he considered himself married to the business and he had no intention of seeking a divorce. For Peter it wasn't about leaving his mark. His legacy would be a history of solid management and strong profitability. He accepted that there was nothing wrong with only doing a good job. Overachievement is overrated. Solid performance stands on its own and most of all stands the test of time.

The company was sound financially and Peter received offers regularly to sell out to large national competitors. TMS was a third generation privately owned company and the thought of selling out was not the least bit appealing to any of the other family members. This business, this facility was Peter's life and up until six hours ago he never questioned that he made all the right decisions.

A large neatly printed sign above one of the oversized parking slots declared that it was reserved for the president of the company. Peter stepped down from his truck and looked around the facility. Several workers instantly noticed him and waved. As he walked to the office, he casually waved back.

The receptionist, Heather Ford, greeted Peter as he entered the main doors to the company's headquarters which was located in a small wood-framed office building near the entrance to the site. "Good morning Peter," Heather said with a broad smile. "Coffee?"

"I'll take it in my office," he responded as he grabbed a stack of pink messages from her desk. He thumbed through them quickly as he walked the long hall to his office. For the first time ever, Peter observed that a strong smell of unburned diesel fuel permeated the building. His sense of awareness seemed heightened today. Maybe Deutsch's call had somehow changed him. Everything seemed different. It was as if he awoke from a long slumber and the world was new again.

As he entered his office, he flicked the light switch then quickly settled in behind his large but plain desk. He removed his cell phone from his belt clip and carefully placed it on the corner of his desk. For a few minutes, Peter sat quietly behind the large desk looking around the office. His grandfather was the previous occupant and conducted business from the very same chair. Peter slowly slid his hand across the rough surface of the desk feeling every dent and imperfection. The finish was well worn and most of the surface was cluttered with mounds of assorted papers, trade publication and correspondence.

His father preached that the money goes into the business and not into high paid consultants, fancy furniture or artwork. The offices at TMS reflected this austere philosophy in spades. No one complained, at least openly so Peter resisted the urge to remodel and update the decor. Plain was all he knew and he had grown comfortable with it over the years. It wore very well. Whenever he thought about remodeling all he needed to do was close his eyes and in the deep recesses of his mind he could hear his grandfather calling for his father.

From out in the terminal, Peter could hear drivers gunning their engines as they pulled their massive rigs onto street. Sitting in his office, detached from the hustle outside, Peter began to realize that he had changed little in the company's business model during his tenure. Maybe his failure to put his mark on the business precipitated the action by the bank. Making some changes was necessary even if they required the expenditure of some of the company's treasure. His father's favorite line was never far from his thoughts...why dabble with success.

Peter was startled from his daydreaming when Heather entered with his coffee. She placed a small paper cup on his desk and stood quietly waiting for Peter to notice her. Paper cups were standard issue at the terminal used by all workers, both in the yard as well as the office. After a few seconds, she decided to speak up. "You seem quiet today."

"I have a few things on my mind," he said casually as he took a sip from the cup. He raised his mug high and continued. "Thanks for the coffee," Peter offered without looking at Heather.

The relationship between Heather and Peter predated her employment with TMS. Heather and Peter met in a local bar and dated heavily for over a year. After she was hired at TMS, they dated for another six months. Eventually they decided that a continued relationship would not survive as long as they worked together. Although they no longer dated, their relationship was special and Peter always gave Heather a little extra attention and latitude in her work.

Peter's lack of attention this day annoyed Heather. "Will there be anything else?" she asked trying her best to show a little attitude. Once again Peter did not immediately respond to Heather's question so she repeated it.

Peter sat up and snapped his orders. "Can we delay our daily scheduling session with the field managers until later today? I have to go downtown with Woody for an important meeting at Union Bank."

"I don't see a problem if you delay the meeting," she replied with a professional swagger. "I will call Mike Turner and tell him to be here after lunch."

"On second thought, Mike knows what the shit he's doing. Call him and only schedule a meeting if he thinks one is absolutely necessary."

"I'll get right on it. I know Bill will be happy to hear that you canceled the meeting today." Heather turned to leave the office. Her skintight jeans caught Peter's attention. Suddenly, she stopped and retrieved a white envelope from under her arm. "I almost forgot," she said returning to the side of the desk. "This envelope was delivered after you left work yesterday. It's addressed to you and stamped urgent." Heather placed the envelope on the corner of the desk then slowly slid it toward Peter displaying her long colorfully painted fingernails.

"Thanks," Peter replied as he grabbed the envelope and held it to read the name of the sender." He tossed it across the desk in Heather's direction. "File it in the Union Bank file," he instructed in a coarse tone.

Heather slowly picked up the envelope and asked, "Aren't you going to open it? It might be important."

"It's damn important, but I already know what it's about. Just file it," he said curtly.

Heather did not respond to Peter's remarks. She stood silently on the side of his desk and after a few moments Peter realized that his harshness had bruised her delicate feelings. Although she worked around a hoard of rough truck drivers, Heather was treated as the company princess by everyone. Peter was quickly acquiring a nasty habit of offending pretty women today. "I'm truly sorry. I know I seem to be acting a little surly today. I didn't sleep well last night." He reached for the envelope and opened it with a swift pull of the drawstring. Inside he found the letter from Deutsch. "Yep. It's what I was expecting," he said as he placed the letter back in the envelope. "Please just file it in the Union Bank folder," he instructed as he placed the envelope on the corner of his desk.

With a broad smile, Heather picked up the envelope and returned to her desk. After Heather exited the office, Peter depressed the message button on his phone. One by one, he listened to nearly a dozen messages. Then he looked through the e-mails on his computer. Nothing in either his e-mails or voicemails seemed urgent. It was now eight o'clock, too early to call Megan. Anyway it was doubtful whether she had time to complete her review of the company's loan documents. He knew there were at least a couple dozen individual documents to review. At the closing two years earlier, the bank's lawyer had loan documents stacked more than a foot high. Besides, Peter was probably the last person in the world she wanted to hear from at this early hour.

To make things right with Megan, he knew he would pay dearly. They fought many times before and always reconciled within a short period. This time, he was hopeful that he hadn't pushed her too far. She was an extraordinary lawyer and more importantly, she was a warm and loving companion. If luck was in his corner, she would treat him to a sound tongue-lashing for his earlier stupidity and deny him her sexual pleasures for a few days. The favorable resolution of this business quagmire was not possible without her total support. Beyond that, Peter knew that he and Megan were meant for one another. Maybe it was time for him to make their relationship permanent.

It was difficult for Peter to concentrate. He continually replayed in his mind the telephone conversation from the previous evening. No matter how much he parsed the conversation, none of it made any sense whatsoever. Why would the bank take the action they did? Surely, they didn't make any money on the deal. They disposed of a valuable earning asset that was over- collateralized and represented no possible risk of loss.

Suddenly, his cell phone sprang to life. He was confident it was Megan with some preliminary results to report. Before the second ring was complete, Peter snatched the phone from his desk and flipped it open to check caller ID. The number of the caller was not displayed so Peter elected not to answer. He continued to hold the phone in his hand as he leaned back in his chair. Maybe it was Megan calling from a different number, one his cell phone didn't recognize. On the other hand, it could be Jeff Deutsch calling with more bad news. Still Peter did not answer the phone. Soon the racket ceased without the caller leaving a voice message.

Peter opened the phone and paged through his phonebook to Megan's office number. He hesitated for a few seconds before he pressed the call button. He wasn't sure what to say, but he knew that if he waited too long before calling her, it would be impossible to deal with her. After five rings with no answer the phone system switched the call to her voicemail. After the beep, Peter said nothing and simply closed his phone to disconnect the line. Then he called her condominium in Four Leaf Towers. Again there was no answer. Either she was avoiding him or she was in transit to work. Peter decided against calling Megan on her cell phone.

The morning activity around the office was in full swing when Peter stepped from behind his desk to visit Woody Coppell. Across the hall from his office, Peter stopped and stared at a closed door leading to another office. Attached to the door right below eye level was a simple nameplate. It was held in place with four well-tarnished brass screws. Behind the door was the office where Peter's father worked for over thirty years. Throughout his tenure with TMS he never once closed the door. After his father's death Peter closed the door out of respect. The nameplate was never removed. Peter only ventured into the office on three occasions since the death of his father, mostly to retrieve important business or family documents. This morning for some unknown reason he felt compelled to once again enter the office. Tentatively, he reached for the knob but before feeling the coldness of the polished brass, he heard someone calling his name from down the hall.

CHAPTER 3

"Ferrell's mad as a hornet," the caller reported with concern peppered in his tone. "I don't think he's going to take this lying down. He's a fighter and I'm concerned that the bank will get dragged into a messy situation."

"Calm down and stop worrying. Everything will be fine. You will see that there's nothing that he can do. This deal was done clean as they come. By Friday night, he'll be out on the street and there will be nothing remaining to fight over. At worst I may have to pay a few dollars out of pocket to make him disappear. Let me assure you that he will never be able to reassemble his company. Besides, if he can somehow pull that rabbit out of the hat, the damage I'm going to do to his reputation will be irreparable and the business will not survive. I can pick up what I want at the auction barn."

"If any stink hits the bank, management will fire me without thinking twice. There is no question in my mind that we moved too quickly on this one. It would have been better to wait another year at a minimum. It's your fault for rushing this sale."

"Another year! Are you insane? You represented to me on several occasions that management at the bank was scared shitless over TMS' loans, didn't you? Now is the right time to strike. In a year, the landscape could be quite different. So stop belly aching. I hate it when you whine. It makes you sound like a pussy."

"I just was thinking..."

"That's your problem. You're not good at thinking. That's my job. Remember I don't pay you to think. I pay you to find profitable deals exactly like this one."

"Still, I'm concerned," the caller warned.

"Concerned about what, your two bit job at the bank?"

"This goes well beyond my job and you know that."

"Your job is working for me and don't you to ever forget that! Besides, what possible reason is there for you to be concerned? Bank executives told you they haven't liked the risk in this deal for a year and you took care of the problem. Heck, once they realize the loan is out of the bank, they'll promote you to senior vice president. After this deal is put to bed, I know you can find many similar deals in your bank's portfolio. I can fund as many as you can scrape together."

"I just don't know if I can keep doing this for you."

The party on the phone tried again to reassure the distressed banker. "You have absolutely nothing to worry about. If they give you any shit, just push it back to their end of the table. Your actions in this matter are legal in every way above reproach."

"There is no question that they will like the fact that the loan is out of the portfolio. My biggest concern is that management at the bank will find out about us," the caller cautioned.

"You will have to make sure that they never make that connection. That's why your compensation is so generous. There is no way they will uncover our relationship as long as you keep your trap shut. Bankers just aren't that smart. And if they do find out about us, I assure I will be very unhappy."

"I agree Ferrell will never figure it out but his lawyer might. She's a damn smart bitch and would like nothing better drill us big time. It's quite possible that either she or Ferrell will show up here unannounced and start asking questions."

"If they do, tell 'em it's out of your hands and refer them to me. I can easily run them around for a couple of days. All we need to do is keep them guessing until the close of business on Friday. I don't think that will be too difficult to accomplish even for you."

"It's the loose ends that I'm worried about. If anything pops up, we're dead!" the caller complained.

"I have taken care of all of the loose ends. Trust me when I tell you that absolutely nothing unexpected is going to pop up."

"If this matter blows up because you were too quick on the trigger, I swear to you I'm not taking any of the heat," the caller threatened.

"I understood that from the start."

※ ※ ※

The summons from down the hall surprised Peter and broke his mental fixation on the door to his father's old office. He stepped back momentarily, collected his thoughts and looked down the hall in the direction of the sound. He saw his chief financial officer standing at the door to his office some thirty feet down the hall. Upon seeing Peter look in his direction, Woody motioned for him to join him in his office.

"Where do we stand? Bring me up to date," Peter called out as he turned from the door to his father's office and slowly ambled toward Woody's office. As the two men entered the office, Peter patted Woody on his back and said, "I really need you to get me out of this jam. I'm counting on you to come through with a home run. This squall has blown in so quickly, I don't know what direction to turn. It wasn't even on the radar screen yesterday."

Woody sat behind his desk while Peter reclined in a large well-worn chair directly in front of the desk. Woody was around ten years older than Peter. He was tall, standing upright at more than six feet. His weight was well distributed so that from a distance he looked far more slender than he was. His brown hair was combed straight back and held in place with copious helpings of styling gel to prevent it from falling across his face. He was divorced and had no children. Over the years Peter observed that Woody seemed to spend most of the daylight hours at work, which no doubt was a contributing factor in his divorce. While he and Peter had known one another for almost fifteen years, they spend no time together outside the office engaged in social intercourse.

The surface of Woody's desk was completely covered with printouts, accounting ledgers, and tightly bound presentations. The unsightly clutter annoyed Peter though he said nothing. He didn't feel that it was his place to admonish his subordinate. Bean counters generally keep their desks neat and organized but that was not Woody. As far as Peter was concerned, what Woody did was Woody's business. Still Peter was not comfortable with the lack of professionalism Woody projected. True Peter's desk was likewise cluttered with paper, but he was the president of the company and rarely spent time in the office. Hanging out in the field was Peter's office, talking to the dispatchers and swooning customers. There was no marketing department at TMS. Business development was always managed out of the back pocket of one of the Ferrell men.

Since taking the reins of the company, Peter rarely consulted Woody on important business matters. Peter saw Woody was good accountant hired by his father to keep the numbers balanced, nothing more. In Peter's opinion Woody did not possess nor demonstrate the business acumen necessary to run a sophisticated multi-state commercial operation. Peter never cared for Woody Coppell's personal style either. At TMS, he was the odd duck out and Peter sensed that Woody liked it that way.

This new threat arising from the bank's sale of the TMS loan caused Peter to reevaluate his reliance on his chief financial officer. This problem involving the company's financing arrangements was now more than Peter believed he could manage alone. Financial matters after all were Woody's bailiwick. It was now time for him to step out from behind his cluttered desk, earn his paycheck and earn it quickly.

"What's the hubbub?" Woody asked his boss. "You called me at half past midnight, and asked me to pull together fresh numbers and gin out a presentation for the bank. Then you babble something about moving our banking relationship. What is going on?"

"That asshole Deutsch from Union Bank called last night clear out of the blue and told me that yesterday the bank sold our note to an outfit out of Chicago called Venture Funding."

"Isn't that Marler McAdams' firm?"

"You know about him?" Peter shot back surprised by Woody's instant recognition of the name.

"You bet. I thought everyone knew about the guy and his questionable tactics."

"What tactics?" Peter asked in surprise.

"Let's just say his unsavory reputation is well earned and he is not someone you want to ride along with for any length of time. Most of his trips are strictly one way."

"I don't want to ride anywhere with Marler McAdams behind the wheel. So you agree that we need to get out of this deal as quickly as possible. I'm thinking we need to convince management at Union Bank to buy back our note, or we need to immediately move to another financial institution. That's the reason I need updated information ASAP."

"Maybe you are moving too quickly," Woody suggested. "Let's take some time to uncover his plans and see if he has a formal timetable for implementation."

"Time is of the essence. Megan is reviewing the loan documents as we speak looking for some out."

Woody tried to calm Peter. "Take a deep breath. I don't think the Venture Funding is going to move against you post haste. The loan is paid current. So all you need to do is just sit back and make your easy monthly payments. Wait for McAdams to call. If he has an agenda, and I bet he does, he will reveal his hand in a few months maybe sooner, but I doubt much sooner."

"I don't want to wait a couple of months. McAdams is a bottom fisher with a nasty reputation. Something in my gut tells me that his agenda is one that none of us will like. I have never heard a positive thing said about that bastard. I need your complete and undivided attention on this matter until it is resolved."

Woody signaled that he understood Peter's position. He wanted a foolproof plan to permanently resolve this dilemma. There was no need to wait for Peter to lay the cornerstone in the foundation of his plan. Woody was ready and outlined his preparations thus far. "Earlier this morning I pulled fresh numbers so that I could prepare an in-depth presentation. If Union Bank doesn't listen to your sales pitch, the other banks in town will need a detailed financial package to evaluate a new loan request of this size. I printed and bound several additional copies and I will have Heather call a courier to deliver them to several banks before we leave for our meeting with Deutsch.

The sooner they have the numbers, the sooner we can negotiate terms and set a closing date. I don't want anything to delay their evaluation of our request to move the company's loan." Woody tossed a copy of the presentation across his desk.

Peter smiled approvingly and snatched the document from the desk. As he thumbed quickly through the freshly printed pages, he nodded. "Great job! I knew you could get this done. How many banks do you think will bid on our business? Three? Four?"

"I am confident that we will receive at least three bids locally. If we are lucky one of the big banks in Dallas will also tender a bid. I've made several calls this morning and have two meetings scheduled for early afternoon. I know you will want to attend each meeting with me. A good sales pitch from the company's chief executive officer will help cement a deal and get it closed quickly."

"That won't be necessary. My schedule will be hectic for the next few days. You know our business as well as anyone and I have all the confidence in your ability to get us where we need to be structurally, low rate and easy monthly payments," Peter said in a confident tone. "I don't think any of those guys want me to pump sunshine up their skirts. It's the hard numbers they will want to thoroughly crunch."

Woody was surprised at Peter's response, especially his unconditional support. He did not immediately respond as he was unsure what he should say. This was the first time in recent memory that Peter was complimentary of his work or acknowledged his contribution to the success of the company.

Peter looked up from the presentation and waited for Woody to continue.

After a few seconds of silence, Woody blurted, "What's your strategy for our meeting with Union Bank?" This was the first thing that popped into his head.

Peter leaned forward in the chair and placed his elbow on the desk. "I'm still formulating my plan of attack. I thought we could drive downtown in about an hour and confront Deutsch. Once he sees our new numbers I know he will realize that Union Bank made a huge mistake selling our loan. It should then be a painless transaction to reverse the sale of our loan and return the documents to Houston. Regardless of whether or not we get his buy-in, I want you to meet the other banks. I will never bank with Union Bank again."

"Do you think the bank would actually repurchase our note?" Woody asked. "Remember they will have to get the buyer to agree. If Venture Funding bought the loan at a discount, which is what I expect, then chances are good that McAdams expects to make a handsome profit."

Peter ignored Woody assessment. "Banks are in business to make money. The sale of TMS' loan was not a good business decision. Once they realize the error of their hasty action, I know that they will want to straighten this whole thing out. They should have no problem canceling the transaction and returning the money to Venture Funding. It is doubtful any of the ownership transfer documents have been filed at the courthouse."

"I hope you're right and the bank gets our loan back. Otherwise it's going to be an expensive proposition moving our banking relationship to another bank. The fees alone will sink our results for the quarter," Woody warned. "Historically business slows this quarter and a large unplanned expenditure will throw us in the red. Under generally accepted accounting principles, TMS can capitalize a large chunk of the refinancing costs, but the financial impact will to the bottom line nonetheless be significant."

Peter closed the presentation and tossed it on Woody's desk. He leaned back in the chair and in a casual tone questioned Woody. "What do you make of all this crap?"

Woody shook his head. "It's how business is done in the 21st century," Woody responded nonchalantly.

"Maybe so. Still, it doesn't add up to me. First the bank sells our note with any notice and then Deutsch pulls his stroke of midnight call. It all smells fishy to me, too cloak and dagger. There is something going on. I just know it. If we press Deutsch, I know we can get him to drop his pants and show us his hidden agenda."

Woody cracked a light chuckle. "I'm not sure I want to see Jeff Deutsch's hidden agenda."

After both men laughed briefly Peter continued. "Banks are a squirrelly lot, especially these days. The damn bank regulators have them scared shitless over loan losses. If they think a loan has any chance of going south, they move it out of their portfolio quickly as they can into the secondary market. If the sale results in a loss, so be it. They don't give a rat's ass about the impact it has on their customer. It's one less loan to fight over at the next FDIC Safety and Soundness Examination."

Woody agreed with Peter's assessment.

Peter once again leaned onto the desk. He placed his elbow down hard and moved his hand to his cheek. He rubbed his face and openly revealed his personal thoughts. "Since the call from Deutsch I keep asking myself over and over, how would my dad handle this situation? I wonder if he ever faced a problem as serious as this one." Peter shook his head from side to side and exhaled slowly.

Woody saw that his boss was visibly upset by the unfortunate turn of events. Peter revealed for the first time a softer side to his personality that Woody had never seen. Maybe he wasn't as rock solid and unyielding as he portrayed.

"I don't know quite what direction to turn. To make matter worse I've gone and pissed-off Megan, the one person I've always been able to count on in tight spots."

"I knew your dad for many years and he always relied on his instincts. You know as well as I do that John Ferrell had great instincts for business. It was like he could smell the right course of action. Then he followed the trail like a Bloodhound. Once he had the scent, he never wavered. Most of all, I remember he never panicked. He rowed his boat one stroke at a time and never looked back. More importantly he never was in a rush to take action. He thought through every obstacle before taking a step."

"No question about it. He didn't let crap like this get under his skin." Peter said admiringly of his father as he then stood and walked to the window. "What do you think I should do about this matter of Union Bank selling our loan?" Peter asked as opened the mini blinds and looked out over the expansive terminal yard.

"Do like your father and don't let it get the better of you. In a couple of weeks this will all blow over and we'll be sitting here laughing our asses off about how we over analyzed the situation to death. I think you're trying to make more of it than there is. In all likelihood this sale is an innocent business transaction nothing more. Together we will get through it. Trust me."

"But what if at the end of the day, it isn't the innocent business transaction that you believe it is?"

"Then you've been had my friend, bent over the desk and screwed rude," Woody piped as he mimicked Groucho Marx.

Peter paced across the room. "I want to believe that you're right. The bank panicked and dumped our loan to the first willing buyer. Something deep inside my gut tells me that there's a snake slithering somewhere in the tall grass. If I can't smoke him out, Megan certainly will. I realize that I'm operating here with an abundance of caution, but I can't afford to play it any other way. I can't let anything happen to TMS. My dad left it to me to shepherd to the next generation. My mother and my Uncle Stuart are counting on me to make the right decisions."

"What's Megan's take on this if I may ask? Surely she has to have an opinion."

Peter threw out his hands. "Lawyers," he complained. "They won't take a position until after they are finished reading all of the documents. She promised me that she would pour through the mound of paper until she found a defect, no matter how insignificant that would give us a viable out. I trust that she is doing her job as we speak. To be honest, we had a small fight last night after Deutsch called. For all I know she's mad as an angry badger and is not doing a damn thing."

Woody roared with laughter. "That's an oxymoron if I ever heard one. There is no such thing as a small fight, especially with your girlfriend. Megan Cedars is a terrific woman; she won't abandon you no matter how naughty you've been. She may be mad as a hornet and will sting the shit out of you, but she will do whatever is necessary to get this matter resolved in your favor. And you can take that to the bank, preferably someplace other than Union Bank."

"Yea, you're right. She'll find the chink in their armor and save my sorry ass yet again."

With the conversation winding down, Woody moved to his computer and typed some numbers into a large spreadsheet. He turned to Peter and asked, "Is there anything else you need? If we are leaving around nine, I have a few additional reports I would like to finish and bring with me."

Peter walked to the door of the office. Before exiting he turned and addressed Woody one last time. "Be in my office ready to leave no later than nine-fifteen."

Back in his office, Peter called Megan and again he got her voicemail. He sat quietly in his office tapping on his desk waiting for the time to pass. During the lull in activity, he decided to make a detailed list of tasks that he needed to complete in the unfortunate event the conversation at the bank didn't end on a positive note. On a white legal pad, he jotted down as many items as he could develop. Toward the top of the list Peter included telephone calls to his mother and uncle. Together they owned fifty-one percent of the company. Peter owned the remaining forty-nine percent. If a legal fight was imminent, they certainly needed to be told. Before long the list exceeded twenty line items. As he was about to finish writing another task on his list, Woody appeared at the door.

"Ready?" he called.

Peter jumped with surprise. He was so engrossed in thought that he failed to hear Woody's heavy footsteps moving down the hall.

The two men exited the offices of TMS and climbed into the cab of Peter's truck. The Cummins diesel roared to life as Peter maneuvered out of his parking place. As he approached the main gate, he cried out, "Crap!"

"What is it?" Woody asked. "Did you forget something?"

"I'm nearly out of gas. I meant to fill up yesterday before leaving, but Megan needed me for a charity dinner at the country club and I was running late. After the dinner, we went to my house. With the shit storm unleashed this morning, I forgot to fill-up on the way in.

We're damn lucky I noticed the gas gauge before we headed out. All we need now is to run out of gas on the toll road!"

"We have plenty of time. Besides Deutsch isn't expecting us so we can't be late."

"Hang on. Let me pull this baby over to the pump."

TMS maintained several diesel tanks on site. While it was more expensive to operate company-owned tanks, it saved considerable time for drivers compared to taking the big rigs to the nearest truck stop. Peter selected a diesel-powered truck for his personal use specifically so that he could avail himself of this convenience.

When Mike Turner, the operations manager at the terminal, observed Peter stopping at one of the pumps, he sprang from his office. "Fill her up?" he asked with a smile.

"No, just put in ten gallons. I'm in a hurry to get downtown for an important meeting. I can top it off later."

"This is a pretty rig Mr. Ferrell. I'd sure like to have one but my wife won't hear of it. She wants a minivan to haul our little rug rats around."

"Fortunately, I don't have that problem," Peter responded with a chuckle.

"I hear ya," he said as he removed the nozzle from the tank. "You should have an easy trip at this hour. When you return, leave your keys with Heather and I'll finish filling her up."

"That's great Mike. I should be back around mid-afternoon at the latest."

CHAPTER 4

The traffic on the Hardy Toll Road was light as Mike predicted. In the distance through the perpetual Houston haze, Peter could make out a cluster of high-rise buildings. As he drove toward the central business district, the famous Houston skyline came into full panoramic view. Peter approached downtown Houston from the north, which is generally considered to be the less dramatic view. The locals prefer the western skyline often voted the most stunning. It is the western skyline that the local organizations selected to market the city.

By the middle of the morning the streets in downtown Houston were virtually deserted with most vehicles out of sight parked tightly in the many multistory garages. Most sidewalks with the exception of those on Main Street were all but devoid of pedestrians. Peter decided to park in the Milam Street parking garage located across the street from Union Bank. The lower floors were full which forced the pair to park on the top floor. They quickly moved to the elevator and once inside Woody pressed the button for the ground floor. Upon exiting the elevator, they stepped onto an escalator for the short ride to the underground tunnel system.

The majority of the downtown office buildings in Houston are joined through a series of underground tunnels. They connect more than thirty blocks, which keeps the thousands of office worker off the streets and out of the notorious Houston heat and humidity. Peter and Woody found the tunnels alive and vibrant, unlike the sidewalks above. As they walked toward the bank, they passed many shops, restaurants and banking offices. The tunnels were especially appreciated on rainy days, which are a Houston staple.

The pair soon arrived at the bank then rode the bank's escalator to the lobby to find the main bank of elevators. The commercial lending department was located on the sixth floor of the forty-story building. In the elevator, the two men found themselves alone. Woody turned to Peter and issued some works of encouragement. "Knock 'em dead champ. Save our company from the rabble."

Peter turned and smiled but gave no response. Inside he was shaking uncontrollably and a swarm of butterflies in his stomach felt like dive-bombers. A loud chime announced the arrival at the sixth floor. Peter held out his arm signaling Woody to exit first. They stepped out of the elevator and into a large yet abandoned reception area. Rather than wait for the receptionist to return, Peter and Woody decided to walk down the hall toward Deutsch's office. It was the third office on the left.

Peter was the first to the door and noticed that Deutsch was on the phone with his attention directed to something on the surface of his desk. He stood motionless for a minute or so leaning against the metal doorframe to the office. Deutsch never looked up from his desk. After a couple of minutes, Peter decided to simply walk into the office. Peter's sudden move into the office surprised Deutsch as he hurried to end his telephone conversation. He held up his hand signaling for his guest to wait, but Peter openly ignored the gesture. Once in the office Peter sat in one of two empty chairs directly across from the desk. He then motioned for Woody to enter.

When the phone call ended Deutsch stood and walked around to the front of his desk. He eased back upon the edge of the desk directly in front of Peter. He leaned forward and in a near whisper addressed his guests. "What on earth are you two doing here? I told you the bank no longer owns your loan. There is nothing for us to discuss."

It was clear that Deutsch was agitated and uncomfortable with the surprise visit. Neither Peter nor Woody said a word and simply stared at their former banker. Deutsch continued to address his unwelcome visitors. "Please leave now. I don't want a scene. Rest assured that I will not hesitate to call security to escort of you from the premises."

Peter spoke next. "Calm down Jeff. We didn't come armed with anything more than the numbers. Woody has put together a great package of new information that I know will change your mind about the quality of TMS' loan. You will see that it was a mistake to sell our loan to Venture Funding." He then motioned for his CFO to discuss the presentation.

Woody handed a package to Deutsch and immediately went into his spiel. "The company posted significant revenue gains over the past three months."

Deutsch turned slightly, placed the financial package hard on his desk then called for a halt to the proceedings. "Please stop. The loan is gone and there is nothing I can do. You are wasting time your time and mine. I don't care what the numbers show."

Peter interjected, "I think the numbers tell an important story."

"For what purpose?" Deutsch demanded as he returned to his chair. "Where are you going with this?"

"To convince the bank to buy back our loan from McAdams of course," Peter explained, his voice growing louder with each word. "I signed a deal with this bank and I expect you to honor that deal. I am not interested in working with a new party at this stage of the game."

"You didn't listen to a single word I said last night and you are not listening to me now," Deutsch said gruffly. "The loan is sold and it's not coming back. Never! Assuming I wanted to buy it back, and I don't, I doubt McAdams would agree to sell it back to the bank even if we offered a premium. Believe me Peter; bank will not pay a premium to repurchase your note. Case closed." Deutsch pointed to the door. "Get out!"

"So what am I supposed to do at this point?" Peter asked beginning to accept the finality of the situation.

Deutsch fumbled among the papers on his desk and retrieved a business card. He flipped it across the desk and addressed Peter in a somewhat conciliatory tone. "Here is McAdams' business card. I probably shouldn't give this to you," he said hesitantly. "Shit, take it and give him a call. I think you'll find him to be reasonable. Your loan is now with him and I'm sure he's more than willing to work with you to do whatever is necessary to keep your company humming along smoothly. After all, he is a reasonable businessman who just shelled out a chunk of change to get his hands on your note."

"That's not his reputation!" Peter barked at the stoic banker. Sensing that he may have pushed the limit and that Deutsch was firmly dug in to his position, he backed down. "I know you're fairly new with the bank and maybe don't fully appreciate the long history between my family and this bank. I see my efforts this morning have been in vain and I'm sorry for taking your time." He motioned to Woody and the two men left without shaking the banker's hand or exchanging further words.

Deutsch followed the two men out of his office and watched as they entered the elevator. Once they departed he returned to his office, closing the door as he entered. Within seconds he was on the phone. "You were correct. Ferrell and Coppell arrived at my office first thing this morning. I just escorted them to the elevator. As you instructed, I gave them your business card. Expect a call later today."

"Good work. You see, everything will flush out quickly. He is doing exactly as I would do. What he doesn't yet understand is that his time is quickly running out. When he does, it will be too late."

"I have always deferred to you in these matters, but I can tell you, Ferrell is not going to stop. He is a man on a mission. I guess I never realized that he is as forceful as he is. I clearly misread him over the past year. A pushover he is not."

"Let me handle him. You don't have the stomach once blood is drawn."

"Are you referring to Cleveland?" Deutsch demanded. "I told you we moved too fast this time. They know all about you and if they somehow learn about Cleveland, we are both going to do time."

"Are you threatening me?"

"You know me too well to expect me to do something so irrational. We have a good thing going and I don't want to see it ruined because of a little greed," Deutsch stressed.

"Our analysis indicated this is a perfect candidate and the profit is incalculable. Greed doesn't come into play. A good deal is a good deal and I'm not passing up the chance for a sizable profit just because you think we moved to fruition at too rapid a pace. That's how this game is played. Speed is absolutely critical to success. If you move too slowly, you lose."

"I agree it's a sweet opportunity. I hope we didn't play our hand too soon."

"Regardless of Ferrell's strategy to keep his company, I'm still holding several trump cards in reserve. He doesn't realize he is playing a game that he has already lost. Keep me informed of any further actions on his part."

✯✯✯

The two men did not speak during their brief ride to the lobby. They only managed to stare at the individual floor numbers as they flickered on the overhead display. Once in the main lobby of the bank, Peter glanced at his watch. It was already eleven-fifteen. He offered to buy Woody a cup of coffee in a café located across from the escalator in the tunnel. There they could discuss next steps.

The pedestrian traffic in the tunnel was building as the lunch hour approached. They each ordered coffee then Peter selected a table in the corner of the café far away from the plate glass window, which created the appearance of a fishbowl. He wanted privacy where he could be as far as possible from the distractions of the frenzied crowd. What Peter really feared was being recognized by someone passing by the café.

Almost immediately upon sitting, Peter jumped up to get creamer for his coffee. Woody flipped open his cell phone and began tapping on the small buttons. When Peter returned to the table, Woody closed the phone, poured sugar in his coffee and began to stir rapidly. "I just checked my voice messages. John Bailey at Houston National can meet at noon and Dave Fields at Texas Merchants is available at two. Once we finish here, I should be able to walk to Houston National within a few minutes. They are anxious to get a peek at our deal. I knew these guys would be hungry to bid on our business."

"That's great news. I have rethought my position after meeting with Jeff and now believe that we should both meet with the banks. They need to hear from the CEO before making a decision on refinancing our loan. It's a sizable transaction and I want to demonstrate to them my passion for the business."

Woody did not look up from his coffee. Peter's suggestion was not what he expected nor planned. "Do you have the time?" Woody asked. "Deutsch told you to call McAdams and ask about his plans for the note. Besides, Megan is probably ready with her initial findings. I can handle the banks," he said in a reassuring tone. "It's best if we work in parallel rather than in lockstep. That way we can cover significantly more ground. This is the first meetings with these bankers. They want to get their arms around the numbers before we feed them our goals for the next decade. I think the best play is to bring them out to the terminal next early week and treat them to a corporate dog and pony show. Let 'em drive a forklift and load one of the trucks."

"Yea, you're right. Divide and conquer," Peter toasted as he downed the last of his coffee. "You go ahead then. I'll call Megan and see how she's progressing. Her office is only a few blocks away. Maybe I'll walk over and see her in person. What time do you want to meet to head back to the office?"

Woody pushed back his chair and picked up his briefcase. "Don't worry about me. I'll get a ride or take a cab. Let's meet later this afternoon back at the office and bring each other up to speed on the latest developments." Woody tossed his empty cup in a trash receptacle as he exited the café.

Peter watched as Woody disappeared into the tunnel system. For a few minutes, he sat quietly at the table. After a second cup of coffee he called Megan's number. This time she answered the phone. "I'm calling to see if you have any information yet?" Peter asked in a subdued tone.

"Nothing," Megan replied coldly. "We have already had several fires around the office this morning. I have reviewed several documents and have asked my paralegal review the others. She is the best document reviewer at the firm. If there are errors, she will quickly find them."

"Do you know anything at this point?" Peter asked. "I'm just grasping for any good news."

"From the few documents I have already reviewed, it appears my files are incomplete. When this loan was renewed two years ago, I know that I asked the bank's attorney for a complete set of documents. Maybe I can call Deutsch and get a complete copy from the bank."

Megan's words were cold and without any hint of emotion whatsoever. Peter sensed that she was still brooding over his rude conduct the previous evening and he fully understood that he had no choice but to ride out her tidal wave of anger. There was nothing that he could say at this time that he believed would improve his plight. He dug the hole, dug it deeper and there was no escape. When Megan was ready to reconcile, he figured she would lay him out flat as a board, and he would have to take the thumping like a man.

"Don't call Deutsch," Peter replied. "I'm in the tunnel below the bank. I'll run back up to his office and pass on your request. If you want I can wait for the copies and bring them to your office. I'd like to spend a few minutes with you discussing strategy."

That was the best reason that Peter could muster for going to see Megan. Over the years, he found that she was much more compliant meeting face-to-face rather than talking over the phone. He hoped he could warm her frosty edges with a quiet meeting.

"Don't bother," she said abruptly. "The service just delivered copies of the county and UCC security filings. I probably can't get to the loan documents until late today or tonight."

Peter thought he sensed an opening in Megan's disposition. He made his move. "I thought we could have dinner at The Palm tonight. I can pick you up from the office."

After a few seconds of silence, Megan responded to his offer. "I'm busy trying to save your ass," she stated without emotion in her tone. Then she hung up the phone.

The biting comments stunned Peter. Never in his three-year relationship with Megan had she been so angry, so cold and for so long. If he didn't get on top of this problem quickly, their relationship, both business and personal, could well be drawing to an untimely end. He closed his cell phone and clipped it to his belt. As he walked out of the café, he crushed his empty coffee cup to vent his frustration then, tossed it in the trash receptacle.

CHAPTER 5

"Jeff," Peter said softly as he once again stood at the door to the banker's office. "Can I trouble you for one last item?"

"What is it?" Deutsch chirped in a harsh tone. "I told you earlier there is nothing further for us to discuss."

Peter bit his tongue as he tried to maintain his composure with his former banker. "Your position was made perfectly clear earlier," Peter acknowledged. "Megan is in the process of reviewing all of the loan documents to identify the rights of the new owner. When I spoke to her a few minutes ago she indicated that her set of loan documents was incomplete. I am here at her request to get a fresh copy from your operations area. If you prefer I can wait in the lobby while they are photocopied."

Peter's submissive demeanor relaxed Deutsch and he dropped his guard. He cracked a minimal smile and responded to the document request. "When we sold TMS' loan to Venture Funding we delivered to them all of the bank's original documents. So we can't make a copy for Megan."

"Well, it was worth a try," Peter replied signifying his acquiescence to the situation. "Megan will have to work with whatever she has." With no more business to discuss Peter turned to leave Deutsch's office. Before he stepped away from the door completely, he once again addressed Deutsch, this time in jest. "Thanks for not calling security."

"Hold on," Deutsch said as he stood and walked to a beige file cabinet wedged in the corner of his office. "I usually keep a copy of loan documents on all my deals just in case I need to look up a loan covenant or something. I get my attorney to charge the cost to the client." He opened the top drawer and removed two large files. "This is what I have on TMS. I can't guarantee it's a complete set, but since you paid for them you can have both files if you want."

Without another word, Peter accepted the two heavy bundles of loan documents and once again rode the elevator to the lobby of the bank. Rather than returning to his truck, he decided to walk the short distance to Megan's office to deliver the documents personally. The temperature on the street was nearly unbearable. The crosswalk signals seemed slow as Peter stood in the bright sun and cooked. Sweat poured from his brow as he entered the main lobby at First City Tower. Megan's office was located on the forty-second floor. Like most law offices, the decor was warm and inviting with muted colors and soft lighting.

The receptionist at Megan's firm immediately recognized Peter as he stepped from the elevator. Her broad smile warmed the room. "Good afternoon Mr. Ferrell. Let me buzz Megan to let her know you are here in the reception area."

"That won't be necessary. She asked me to get these files and since I was in the neighborhood, I thought I could drop them off. I know it can get hectic around here and since she is not expecting me please don't bother her."

"Don't be silly. I know that she always has time for you," the receptionist responded with a quick wink followed by a smirk. "Let me ring her office."

Before the receptionist pressed any numbers into her phone, Megan appeared in the waiting area carrying a handful of files. Upon seeing Peter, she stopped dead in her tracks. Neither said a word for at least ten seconds. They stared intensely at one another, both remaining expressionless.

The uncomfortable silence was broken when the receptionist spoke. "Hey, there you are. Peter came by to drop off some files. I was just about to call you when you came around the corner. It must be great to be in love. You sense when the other is near."

Megan motioned for the two to move away from the hallway where associates of the firm passed continuously. She also wanted to be out of earshot of the receptionist. She pointed at two small chairs in the corner of the waiting room, which were located far from the elevators. Megan spoke first. Her tone was warm but openly restrained.

"I told you it was not necessary for you to bring the files to me. The bank could have couriered them over later."

"The bank doesn't have the original files any longer," he reported. "They gave them to McAdams when he bought the loan. Well, that's what Deutsch claims." As he offered Megan the files he held in his hands, he continued speaking softly as if at a funeral. "These are Deutsch's personal files. They may not be complete, but you can have them if they help. I think he wants to be as far away from this transaction as possible."

"He should crawl under the nearest rock and hide," Megan said in a curt tone as she accepted the files from Peter. "Their actions in this matter are reprehensible. If this story doesn't have a happy ending, at a minimum I think I'll sue them for lender liability. It might be a tough case, but I'm so mad at those bastards, I'll do anything. I don't need this headache right now."

Megan stood and started to return to her office. "I'll get my paralegal to inventory these documents and crosscheck them against what I have in my files. I hope that these records are more inclusive and between both sets I can reconstruct a complete record of the loan. If I find anything significant I will call you immediately."

Peter grabbed her arm and stopped her retreat. "Can we talk," he asked tenderly. "I know I've acted poorly and you have a right to be angry."

Megan did not resist Peter's hold and turned to address her client. "I'm not ready to talk," she stated coldly. "Living with you is like living on a roller coaster. You are constantly moving up and down. At first I liked the excitement, but frankly in recent years I've grown tired of it all. I never know who will show up, you or your evil twin. And I don't much care for that bastard."

Peter hung his head. After a few seconds, he raised his eyes until they met hers. "Megan, you are the most important person in my life. I will do whatever you want to keep this relationship together. When this blows over, I want us to get back to normal."

In rapid succession, Megan jabbed her index finger into Peter's chest. "That's the crux of the problem in our relationship Peter. You want the right to suspend the rules of civility whenever there is a crisis. I can't do that. With me, what you see is what you get. I work hard to maintain a steady state disposition."

"What's wrong with suspending the rules in emergencies?" Peter barked starting to raise his voice. "I have a lot at stake here and I want to protect it all."

"I'm fine with suspending the rules on certain occasions, rare occasions. Since I have known you, the rules have been continuously suspended. And when they are, you are impossible to live with."

Peter's blood pressure instantly rose and his face turned a bright red color as he addressed Megan. "What do you want me to do? I need your help. I thought I could do this along, but it is looking like I can't. I'm so turned around and upside down, I don't know what direction is up."

"Okay," Megan responded as she calmed slightly. "Go ahead and call McAdams in Chicago. See if you can figure out what that son of a bitch is planning to do with your loan. I doubt he will tell you anything, but who knows. Maybe he is so confident in his position that he just might tell you everything. It is worth a shot. Besides, you aren't doing anything but walking around with your thumbs up your ass. If you need me, I'll be in my office reviewing documents." Without another word, Megan left Peter standing alone in the far corner of the waiting room.

Their loud racket attracted attention with several associates who stepped from their offices to stare at the unhappy combatants. Peter felt like a schoolboy sternly admonished by his favorite teacher. For the next few minutes he stood alone shaking his head. Then he returned to the elevators to leave. Megan's words stung him hard. He was not ready to throw in the towel, but he realized she was correct on every point. Patching his relationship back together with Megan was turning out to be a monumental undertaking.

As he passed the receptionist on his way to the elevator, she smiled and remarked, "Isn't love wonderful?"

Peter drew a deep breath but neither looked in her direction nor responded to her remarks. He wanted to get off the forty-second floor as quickly as humanly possible.

Peter returned to his truck and gathered his thoughts. In the quietness of the cab his problems didn't seem to exist and he rested his head on the soft headrest. Soon the stress left his body. He retrieved Marler McAdams' business card from his wallet and fumbled with it momentarily. Then he opened the cell phone and called the number printed at the bottom of the card. As he waited for Venture Funding's receptionist to answer, he replayed in his mind all of his earlier conversations with Megan. Peter was in another time zone, another universe, when his call was answered by a heavy but slimy smooth voice.

"Mac speaking, what can I do for you?"

Peter did not say a word. He remained silent for almost fifteen seconds. "Marler," Peter finally said with surprise in his voice. "I didn't expect you to answer your phone."

"Who the hell did you expect to answer my phone?" McAdams asked with a pronounced gruff.

"I expected your receptionist to answer your phone."

"She's not here right now," he grunted. After a momentary pause he continued. "Who the fuck is this anyway, I don't have all day to play these games."

"This is Peter Ferrell calling from Houston," Peter replied trying to push some sunshine in Marler McAdams' direction. "I trust this is a good time to call. Jeff Deutsch at Union Bank here in Houston suggested we get together to discuss your company's recent purchase of their note from Transportation Management Services. I would think that you want to quickly understand the details of the trucking business."

McAdams' tone immediately changed for the better. The jagged edge in his voice immediately disappeared replaced by a silky smooth rhythm. "I've been waiting for your call Peter. I believe it is critical for the two of us to meet as soon as possible to discuss the future of your company. Can you fly to Chicago tonight so we can meet tomorrow? I know this is an exciting time for both of us."

"Marler, I'm really busy right now. We are moving into the peak of the shipping season and I'm hard pressed to find any available time to fly up to Chicago. Is it at all possible that I can put off the trip until next week, maybe the following week? I think it is important for my chief financial officer to also meet with you so that he can provide you with a complete briefing on the numbers. A meeting in a couple of weeks would even be better."

McAdams did not immediately respond to Peter's counteroffer. He allowed the silence to linger for nearly a full minute. Finally, when he felt his point was made, he cleared his throat. "You surprise me Peter Ferrell. I understood from Deutsch that you are extremely angry over my purchase of your loan and I thought you would want to quickly establish a close working relationship with my organization. It is your decision if you decide to put off a meeting for several weeks. Let me just say I will be gravely disappointed if you do."

Peter knew he was cornered. He should have taken a few minutes to prepare for his first encounter with Marler McAdams. He thought he could wing it on a phone call, but his adversary was far too shrewd. It was clear to Peter that he was wrong to discount the man's nasty reputation as a tough take no prisoners adversary. Maybe Megan was correct when she said that his clumsy tactics don't work as well as he thought. Peter stumbled far too easily into McAdams' well-laid trap before he was alert to what was happening. He reluctantly acknowledged the loss of the first round acquiescing to McAdams' demands. "My assistant will book me on a flight tonight. Can you recommend a hotel near your office?"

"I know you will not regret your decision. I will have my secretary call Heather with all the details. Plan to be my office sometime near noon and we will lunch before getting down to business."

"Would you like me to bring my chief financial officer? He recently prepared a detailed presentation on my company and I think it will be of great benefit to have the three of us meet."

"Leave Coppell at home," McAdams instructed. "Bring the numbers and we can review them during our meeting. I am anxious to understand how my investment will perform over the next few years."

"I will see you tomorrow," Peter responded in an upbeat tone.

McAdams disconnected the call without another word said. Peter closed his cell phone, started his big rig and sped home to pack for the trip. As he pulled into his driveway, he glanced at his watch. It was already three o'clock. Since this trip to Chicago was only for one night, it wouldn't take Peter long to pack. Everything he required folded neatly into a medium L.L. Bean duffle bag. Peter preferred this size carry-on because it easily fit in any airplane overhead bin and security rarely checked its contents.

After he completed packing, he crawled back into his truck for the return to TMS' terminal. He once again opened his cell phone, this time he called the office. "Heather. I need you to book me a trip to Chicago."

Before he could finish dictating his instructions, Heather interrupted. "It's all done," she reported. "You leave Bush Intercontinental at seven from gate forty-two in Terminal C on a Continental flight, non-stop to O'Hare," Heather reported to her boss. "You return to Houston on the six o'clock direct flight on Wednesday."

"As usual your attention to detail is perfect." Peter said to compliment his office manager.

"Oh, I didn't do anything. Maggie called me with all of the details."

"Who is Maggie?" Peter demanded.

"She's Mr. McAdams' office manager," Heather disclosed to her surprised boss. "And I must say that she is extremely friendly. I think I will like working with her."

"Fine, give me the details again."

Heather repeated Peter's itinerary.

"I don't think I will need that much time with McAdams," Peter observed. "I can't imagine we will have that much to discuss. Get me on an earlier flight back to Houston."

"Maggie was very specific about your flight times," Heather stressed in her effervescent tone.

"Where am I staying?"

"You have a reservation at the Hilton downtown. It's near Venture Funding's office."

"How do you know it's near their office?" Peter inquired.

"Maggie told me. In fact, she handled everything and called with your itinerary. Venture Funding is even footing the bill."

"How did she know to call you?"

"I don't know but she said that you and Mr. McAdams were in agreement with the schedule," Heather informed Peter. "I hope I didn't do anything wrong."

"No it's fine. It just seems too organized."

"Maggie said that they want your trip to be perfect. I told her that you have never been to Chicago."

"I don't think I will have any free time for sightseeing."

"Are you on your way back to the office?" Heather asked.

"Yes. I've been by the house to pack for the trip. I'm about fifteen minutes from the office. Has Woody returned?"

"He got back about ten minutes ago. He didn't call you because he thought you might be with Megan."

"Tell Woody I want to see him when I arrive. Then call Megan and give her my itinerary. She always wants to know anytime I leave town."

It was late in the afternoon when Peter finally arrived at the terminal. The shadows were long and many drivers scrambled to get their big rigs moving to make the last runs of the day. In the office, Peter walked directly to Woody's office and addressed his chief financial officer. "Where do we stand with the other banks?" he asked as he relaxed in one of the chairs to catch his breath. "Before I meet with McAdams I want to know how my options stack up."

"Both meetings went well," Woody reported with excitement in his voice. "After we separated I first met with John Bailey at Houston National Bank. He thinks they can have an answer within a week. He says our name has come up many times in marketing meetings, but management at Houston National always assumed we were locked in too tight with Union Bank. They assumed that we would never entertain an offer from another bank, even for a better deal."

"How little did they know about our true relationship with those bastards at Union Bank? Shit, we didn't know how bad it was," Peter said tersely. "Does Bailey think they can take the whole deal or will we have to wait from them to sell an over line to other banks?"

"No, they can want to keep the whole deal, all twenty-two million."

"That's great," Peter nearly shouted as he moved close to the desk. He continued. "Why will it take them a week to review our request? Doesn't anyone in that bank have sufficient lending authority to approve our deal on the spot?"

"You know how these banks operate. Everything must go to their loan committee. They first have to perform their due diligence, prepare a credit package and make a formal written presentation to the committee. And remember the committee only meets once a week."

"If we ran our business like the bank runs theirs, we would have folded our tent long ago," Peter quipped. "What does the second bank think they do for us? Who was it, First Energy Bank?"

"Texas Merchants Bank," Woody said with a chuckle. "There's no First Energy Bank in town."

"I know there isn't. The good news is making me feel better already. So what did they say?"

"Dave Fields told me that they liked what I showed them. He really thought the presentation will help him run it through their credit committee that next meets on Friday. If it's a yes, they can close no later than the end of the following week."

"I'm surprised that they can move on the documentation so quickly."

"I think he plans to buy the paper from Venture Funding and re-file all the liens. That will make short work of bringing the loan back to Houston."

"That's great Woody," Peter announced proudly. "I knew you could pull this off without so much as breaking a sweat."

"It's your company and it's a great success story," Woody reminded Peter. "It sells itself."

Peter stood to leave then turned around to once again address Woody. "Oh, I almost forgot. I'm going to Chicago tonight so I can meet with Marler McAdams tomorrow. I'll deliver several of your financial packages so he will lighten up and give us the time we need to move this deal. He sure seems to know plenty about us."

"What do you mean? Well his secretary arranged my trip and called Heather with all the details. I never gave McAdams Heather's name."

"Maybe that asshole Deutsch gave him names and phone numbers. In addition, all of our contact information was probably in the bank's files that Venture now has. I wouldn't worry about it. I think you are just overreacting to the stress."

"Yea, you're probably right."

"By the way, what is your strategy for dealing with McAdams?" Woody asked, "His reputation is that of one difficult and demanding taskmaster who wants his way. He doesn't compromise when it comes to what he wants."

"I intent to shove him the numbers until he chokes on them then tell him we plan to move the loan in short order. What else can he possibly demand?" Peter asked confidently. "Oh by the way, I almost forgot to ask. What rate did you negotiate from the banks?"

"I didn't know you cared about interest rates. I understood that my marching orders were to save the company at all costs."

"Save the company but squeeze them on rates as always."

"One bank offered a great rate tied to LIBOR while another bank wants a floater tied to their prime rate. Both work within our current budget number so long as the spread is razor thin. I'll get you the best deal."

"I know you will," Peter responded. "See you when I return."

"Good luck! I surely hope you don't need it."

Peter leaned on the doorframe and shook his head from side to side. "I hate borrowed money."

CHAPTER 6

In the hectic atmosphere of the lobby bar at the downtown Chicago Hilton, Peter gingerly nursed a Bombay Sapphire and tonic. In the last year Peter found himself increasingly turning to alcohol to help him relax and forget about the demands of running a large multi-state transportation company. This night, he hoped the gin could work its special magic once again. In his private world at the corner of the bar, Peter was almost completely unaware his surroundings. A frenzied rush of patrons moved rapidly through the bar with few spending any appreciable amount of time. It was strictly a business crowd, well experienced in downing their favorite libations while closing the last important business deals of the day.

The flight from Houston to Chicago departed late and ran into severe weather, which prevented food service. With his head pounding, Peter attempted to prepare for his upcoming meeting with Marler McAdams. Based on what he already knew of McAdams' seedy reputation, he fully understood it was essential for him to quickly gain complete control over the meeting and box in his adversary. This was the only way he could expect to successfully manage the relationship until the company's loan was moved to another bank.

Peter was still unable to comprehend any possible reason why Venture Funding opted to acquire TMS' loan from Union Bank. He remained confident that he possessed the finesse necessary to get McAdams to open up and disclose his reasons behind the purchase. This critical information should provide Peter with needed insight regarding his intents in managing the relationship. Although Peter dreaded the possible impact this knowledge represented, he desperately wanted the storms cloud of mystery and uncertainty to dissipate.

As one hour passed into two and two into three, the drinks began to have the desired effect. Peter rested his elbows on the smooth cool surface of the bar and cradled his aching head in palms of his raised hands. Slowly and delicately, he messaged the sides of his temples to drive away what remained of his headache.

From his right, Peter heard someone speak to him. "First time to Chicago?" He rotated his head in his hands and looked in the direction of the voice. "Must be terrible being all alone in such an exciting city? I would really hate to be all by my little lonesome."

Peter slowly lifted his head from its comfortable cradle and spun around on his stool. The first glimpse he caught of the interloper was that of a sparkling faux jewel suspended at the end of a long pendant. As he continued to stare at the pendant for a few moments, he soon realized that it was suspended innocently in the center of a deep v-shaped cleavage formed by what he estimated to be a pair of medically enhanced breasts. The black fabric of the woman's dress strained to contain her significant assets. Peter did not utter a response to the woman's remarks because with several gin and tonics under his belt his mind was completely blank.

The woman moved her right hand from the edge of the bar, reached down into her cleavage and grasped the gold chain of the necklace. She then seductively swung the pendant in a hypnotizing motion to secure his undivided attention. "Mind if I join you?" she purred. "I hate drinking alone."

Still Peter said nothing. His mind raced in a silent fog which slowed his ability to bring rationality to his surroundings. "Sure," he eventually replied stumbling over such a basic response. "Help yourself to any seat that suits you," Peter quipped as he pointed to an adjacent stool. "It's an open bar and you are welcome to sit wherever you please."

She released the chain of her necklace from her petite fingers and laughed in as fake a laugh as Peter ever heard. In one smooth motion she carefully slid onto the stool. No attempt was made to display any modesty whatsoever. Peter was treated to an unfettered view of her working assets. There was no question that she was advertising heavily and wanted Peter to inspect the merchandise in anticipation of closing the deal.

In the dimly lit bar, Peter gave the woman the once over and estimated she was in her early thirties. Street-wise and strictly professional were her calling cards. He laughed under his breath as he addressed his new friend. "Frankly young lady, I don't think you spend very much time alone. From your looks, I bet your dance card is always full."

The young woman laughed coyly at Peter's sophomoric remarks. She opened her small purse and retrieved a long slender cigarette. For a few minutes, she twirled it in her fingers like a majorette's baton. When she was certain she had Peter's undivided attention, she seductively placed the cigarette on her bottom lip and slowly closed her lips together. Upon seeing a regular customer move up to the bar and pull out a cigarette, the bartender drew near the couple. In an instant, his lighter was out of his pocket and with one swift flick, produced a small flame for Peter's guest. She reached over, grasped the bartender's arm and pulled to flame toward the end of her cigarette. After one deep drag, a cloud of white smoke drifted from her slightly parted lips. The bartender put the lighter away and spoke to the woman. "What will you have?" he asked.

She placed her order with business like precision. "Vodka martini, very dry," she swooned in a silky voice. Never once did she look at the bartender or thank him for the light.

It was a sophisticated drink for a sophisticated woman. Peter motioned to the bartender to add her drink to his tab. He decided to have some fun with this young professional in hopes the levity would reduce the unbearable stress. "Come here often?" he asked as he flashed a broad smile in the woman's direction. "You certainly know your way around a bar."

"Are you trying to pick me up?" she purred as she reached up and once again seductively toyed with her pendant. "I've been here once or twice. Is it important for you to know such things about me?"

"Let's say I'm curious about the people with whom I associate," Peter said with a boyish grin growing across his face.

"I'll bet you are curious," she purred. "Be a doll and slide that ashtray over here," she asked as she took one last drag of her cigarette before crushing it out in the ashtray.

After she had fondled with her pendant for a few minutes, she moved her hand up on the chain of her necklace as she once again put the pendant into motion. Peter's eyes were immediately drawn to the woman's substantial cleavage as this temptress slowly stroked her hand up and down the chain then once again reached for the pendant. Slowly she fondled the pendant in a brazen attempt to arouse Peter. It was clear that she was highly experienced in holding a man's undivided attention. When he looked up and his eyes met hers, an evil smile coursed across her face. "Are you available?" he asked innocently as if he didn't know the answer.

At that moment, the bartender returned with her drink. She reached for the stem of the glass and moved the martini close to the edge of the bar. With her elbow resting on the bar, she methodically stirred the drink using the cheap plastic sword, which skewered two large stuffed olives. After the drink was sufficiently stirred, she removed the olives from the glass and placed them near her mouth. Slowly she ran her tongue seductively around each olive then placed the open end of one olive in her mouth and gently sucked the small quantity of alcohol from the inside. When she was certain Peter took the bait, she casually dropped the olives on the bar, picked up her drink and downed it in one quick swill.

"Yes, I am very much available this evening. In fact, tonight I'm here just for you," she responded as she slowly opened her mouth and slid her tongue from one side to the other. "I can make your first visit to Chicago one you will never forget." She then moved her hand to Peter's thigh and massaged it softly. The electricity of her touch excited Peter. Ever so gradually she moved her hand higher and higher on his leg.

Peter cleared his throat. "How much do fond memories cost these days?" he asked as he signaled the bartender to bring fresh drinks. "I don't think I brought enough cash on this trip. It's only an overnight stay."

"Let's not discuss nasty old finances. I told you, I'm here for your enjoyment. Tell me exactly what you want me to do to you for the remainder of the evening."

"Do you have any suggestions? I'm somewhat new at this," Peter confessed with an innocent tone. "You know...never been to the big city before."

"Oh Peter," she cried. "You are such a tease. You big macho boys like to act as if you don't have a clue. Trust me; by noon tomorrow, you will have a much broader view of the world."

The look of total surprise flashed across Peter's face. "How do you know my name?" he asked the young woman in surprise. "I never gave it to you."

"I told you, I've been sent here to take care of your needs," she responded as she moved her hand even higher on his thigh. She leaned in so close to Peter that even in the dim light of the bar he saw that she was absolutely exquisite with no imperfections to be seen whatsoever. There was not even a single smudge of makeup on her face. She didn't need it. The woman was definitely top drawer in every respect, a walking wet dream.

"Someone paid you to come here!" Peter responded. "Who would do such a thing?"

"I don't reveal my benefactors," she shot back her tone more abrupt. "Let's just say I have been well compensated and will do everything you want until you say stop."

The bartender returned with a fresh Bombay and tonic, and a vodka Martini. Peter grabbed his drink and consumed it in one large gulp. He slammed the glass on the bar and called for the bill. When it arrived, he glanced at it briefly, pulled his money clip from his pocket and tossed one hundred dollars on the bar.

"Thank you for the entertainment," Peter said to the woman then turned to leave. "You gave me the release I needed. You are very good."

"What's your room number?" the call girl asked as she slid from the stool. "I'll meet you in your room in a few minutes. Management here at the hotel frowns whenever I accompany my companions to their rooms."

"This is the end of our evening," Peter replied. "I have a busy day tomorrow and I think you can do better than me," Peter insisted as he walked away from the bar.

"Don't leave," she pleaded as she grabbed his arm in an effort to restrain him. "I told you, I'm here for you. There is no need to pay me."

"That's very kind of you, but I'm tired and don't need any company for the evening."

Without any further conversation, Peter walked directly from the bar to the elevator. In his room, he undressed, showered and crashed.

"Good morning, my name is Peter Ferrell and I have an appointment with Mr. McAdams," Peter announced as he entered the door to Venture Funding's offices. "Please inform Mr. McAdams that I have arrived."

"But you're here early," the surprised receptionist confided. "We didn't expect you for several hours. I'll inform Maggie of your arrival. Please wait here."

Peter watched as the attractive young receptionist walked quickly down the hall then turned to her left into one of the interior offices. Before she entered the office completely, she stopped, turned and glanced back at Peter. He could hear her talking to someone in the office. When she did not immediately return, Peter looked around the reception area and selected a chair, which provided him with an unobstructed view down the hall. From where he sat, he was able to see into several of the working areas within the company. While the décor was subtle and unobtrusive, the offices reeked of coldness. There was nothing warm and inviting about Venture Funding. The atmosphere was hard and reminded Peter of a public hospital ward in a large city.

After a few minutes, Peter heard the conversation down the hall starting to wind down. Suddenly, the receptionist reappeared in the hall and returned to her desk. She looked briefly in Peter's direction as she sat at her desk but said nothing. He thought this odd, but decided to say nothing. After all, he was a guest and did not want to begin his relationship with Venture Funding on a sour note.

As the time passed, Peter observed no movement within the areas in his line of vision. He sat quietly rapping his fingernails on a small table next to his chair. Soon he tired of the wait and glanced down at his watch. He had been sitting for nearly twenty minutes. After a couple more minutes passed, movement down the hall caught Peter's attention. A tall, distinguished looking older woman stepped out of an interior office and walked toward Peter. "Why you must be Peter Ferrell," she said as she entered the waiting room. "I'd recognize you anywhere." She confidently extended her hand and introduced herself. "My name is Maggie Lofton and I must tell you that your office manager Heather is a wonderful young lady. She described you perfectly," Maggie stated in a smooth inviting voice. "Even though we only spoke briefly, I could tell that she really admires you and enjoys working for your company."

Peter ignored Maggie's efforts to offer a warm welcome. He was at Venture Funding offices for business, nothing more. "I'm here to meet with Marler McAdams," he informed her with a bite in his voice. "I realize I'm a little early. I trust he is available to see me immediately."

"We expected you much later. But that's not a problem," Maggie replied in her same soft inviting tone. "Mr. McAdams just went into an important meeting and I don't expect that he will be out for at least several hours. There will be time for the two of you to meet when that meeting concludes. In the meantime, he asked that you meet with our controller. So let me take you to meet with Mr. Johnson."

Maggie directed Peter to follow her down the hall but he refused to budge. "Is something wrong?" she asked.

"I didn't come here to meet with your controller. I came here to meet with Marler McAdams," Peter said sternly.

"And yes you will meet with him later. But first you will meet with Terry Johnson," Maggie ordered, her tone much firmer. "So follow me."

As the two entered an office near the end of the hall, the occupant acknowledged Peter arrival. "Glad you could come to see us on such short notice," Johnson barked. "I know this is coming at you fast, but that's the way we work around here." He stepped from behind his cluttered desk and grabbed Peter's hand. After shaking it furiously, he pointed to a small wooden chair and ordered Peter to sit.

"Terry," Peter stated firmly, "What is your position with this firm?"

In a jovial voice Johnson answered Peter. "I like to say I'm the chief cook and bottle washer around here, but I think my card says I'm Mac's controller."

Johnson's weak attempt at humor did not change Peter's sour demeanor. He was angry that he was not immediately taken to Marler McAdams' office. Further, he was more than happy to let the controller endure the brunt of his discontent. Without any inflection in his voice, Peter addressed his host. "What do you want from me? I understand Marler is busy right now."

If Johnson sensed any anger in Peter's tone, he didn't let on. The meeting was arranged for a purpose and nothing was going to divert him off his agenda. He moved to a small table in the corner of his office, opened a Thermos and poured a large cup of coffee. He offered coffee to Peter, but he declined. "Mac is always busy. He's the first true 24-7 person I've ever known." Johnson returned to his desk and took a long swig of his coffee. "I understand from Mac that you have a detailed financial package for us. I am willing to use as much time as necessary to go through Woody's materials to make sure I understand all aspects of your operations. Mac will have a thousand questions later and I don't want to be tracking you down for the answers."

Peter removed several copies of Woody's handiwork and tossed them onto Johnson's desk. "This tells you all you need to know," Peter stated firmly. "If you want anything additional, call Woody Coppell, my chief financial officer in Houston. His phone number is printed on the first page."

Peter detected a change in Johnson's demeanor. "Is there something wrong Mr. Ferrell? Venture Funding just made a huge investment in your company and I sense you are not pleased with our support of you and your company."

The controller's remarks were all that Peter needed to pop his cork and vent. "You're damn right I'm not pleased," Peter snapped. "I didn't ask you to buy my note from those shit asses at Union Bank. I assure you that Marler McAdams and Venture Funding haven't done me any favors whatsoever. And as you can no doubt deduce, I'm thoroughly pissed that I'm in here cooling my jets with you. I came to see Marler McAdams, not his fucking flunky. Venture Funding doesn't own my company. The only asset you own is a promissory note secured by liens and mortgages on my company's assets. That promissory note by the way is and has always been paid current. Venture Funding is a creditor and nothing more. Unlike you I don't report to Marler McAdams. This is a fucking courtesy visit and I believe I should be treated with a little more respect."

Peter was sure that his outburst would catch Johnson off-guard. Unfortunately Peter was wrong. Johnson seemed completely unfazed by Peter's pathetic showboating antics.

Without even the slightest reaction, Johnson continued. "This is the first we have seen of your numbers. Union Bank's files were poorly documented and all of the financial statements on file were seriously outdated. That useless loan officer at the bank, what's his name, Deutsch, wasn't much help. Mac will see you after I'm satisfied that the numbers are accurate and complete. So sit there and how did you put it, cool your jets!"

Peter's anger with Johnson stood at maximum. Beads of cold sweat formed on his forehead. For a few seconds he thought about walking out of the office and into a cab to the airport. Then he remembered Megan's admonishment earlier. If there was a time to remain cool, calm and collected, this was surely it. Pulling a sophomoric vanishing act now would accomplish nothing and certainly get him off on the wrong foot with McAdams. Peter wanted this visit to go off without a hitch and not put the Venture Funding boys on the defensive. If for some reason TMS' loan could not be moved quickly, Peter could be in bed with these jackals for weeks if not months.

The two men sat in the office for about two hours, each saying nothing. Johnson thumbed through Woody's presentation and occasionally tapped numbers into a small calculator. Peter found it difficulty to keep his composure reined in, but he adhered to Megan's advice. Today, he would not be a hot head. He would keep the bad Genie in check and let Johnson and McAdams make the first moves.

When he was finished with his analysis, Johnson closed the presentation with a quick flip and tossed it to the corner of his desk. "Looks like we made a very sound decision to invest in your company," he said with a chuckle. "Performance over the past eighteen months is excellent."

"You didn't make an investment, you bought a note," Peter insisted once again.

As he did with each of Peter's previous comments Johnson did not react. "Look Peter, think of this as a partnership." Then he picked up the telephone and made a call. "He's ready," he reported to his guest. After hanging up the phone, Johnson stood and walked around his desk. He then directed Peter to the door. "Mac will see you now."

Without uttering any response, Peter stood and followed Johnson down the hall. As they walked in locked step, Johnson leaned over and spoke to Peter. "By the way, he likes to be called Mac. McAdams is okay, but he hates Marler with a passion."

"I'll take it under advisement," Peter responded tersely.

At the end of the hall, the two men entered what Peter determined was McAdams' private office. As he looked around the office, he noted that McAdams was not present. "Have a seat and Mac will be with you shortly," Johnson instructed as he turned and walked toward the door.

"You're not joining us?" Peter asked.

"My work is done. Mac wants a one-on-one to discuss his plans for your company."

"His plans, he has plans for TMS?"

Johnson said nothing further, turned and exited the office. Peter sat in a large chair across from McAdams' desk and retrieved his cell phone from his belt. For a second, he thought about calling Megan but he was not sure what he would tell her. So far, he had nothing to report. The meeting with Terry Johnson was a total bust. Peter was optimistic that the impending meeting with McAdams would be enlightening.

Suddenly, a door in the corner of the office opened and a tall athletic build man stepped into the room. From his looks Peter estimated that he was around fifty-five years of age. He walked quickly to where Peter was sitting, thrust out his hand and spoke in a booming voice. "Mac McAdams. You must be Peter Ferrell."

Peter grabbed McAdams' hand. "It's good to finally meet you Mac. I know you have many questions and..."

"Man I'm hungry as a bear. Let's walk down the street to my favorite pub and grab lunch. I think Maggie made a reservation for us."

Before Peter replied to McAdams' offer, he had already walked out of his office. Peter struggled to follow and within seconds the two men were out of Venture Funding's offices without saying another word to one another. In the elevator, Peter attempted some polite conversation, but McAdams paid little attention. He chatted with several members of his staff who shared the ride down.

In the lobby of the building, McAdams stepped quickly from the elevator and out the revolving doors of the building. He took long strides down the sidewalk and Peter found it difficult to keep pace. About two blocks away, they stepped through the doors to local eatery. Peter had hoped for a private club where they could meet in a quiet relaxed atmosphere. The street pub McAdams selected was far too public. The music was extremely loud and Peter realized it would make it difficult to think much less carry on a coherent conversation with his new partner.

That's when it hit Peter like a ton of bricks. He now understood Venture Funding's program clearly. McAdams specifically selected this restaurant because it would be impossible to carry on a conversation. His opponent's strategy was becoming readily apparent. He was a master of the stall and delay. The various stages of his program were falling into place, the hooker, Terry Johnson's reference to McAdams' investment along with a tangible plan for TMS. There was no question about it; McAdams didn't want to hear what Peter had to say. The meeting with Terry Johnson was a well-orchestrated diversion to kill time. While Peter understood the program, he was still unable to decipher McAdams' plan for TMS' future.

From Peter's perspective, Venture Funding was locked into Union Bank's loan deal tight as a drum. As long as TMS made the payments on the note, Venture Funding was shelved from taking any action whatsoever. If Venture Funding bought the TMS note at a discount, then all it would receive was a slightly enhanced return over and above the contractual bank deal. Unfortunately, Peter knew that companies like Venture Funding were not in business to make slightly enhanced returns. They were in it for a killing.

For nearly two hours, McAdams talked about sports and the legs on every woman in the restaurant. Between massive bites of his hamburger, he downed large gulps of a dark lager beer. Not once did he mention TMS or reveal his intentions. Peter opted not to bring up business matters preferring to let McAdams broach the subject when he was ready.

The developing problem for Peter was that it now appeared that McAdams was not going to reveal his agenda. Soon, Peter began to fear that McAdams' agenda might stay hidden indefinitely. So why then was McAdams so insistent that Peter make the hurried trip to Chicago? Peter accepted that his host was a big man with a tremendous ego and he would have to wait until he was ready to show his hand.

It was nearly three o'clock when Peter and McAdams departed the restaurant and returned to his office. By this time Peter was suffering from a pounding headache. Between the cold beers, loud music and unbearable tension, it was bound to happen. McAdams sat behind his desk and continued to ramble from one useless topic to another. Peter kept looking at his watch, he needed to get the discussion moving to the meatier matters if he was going to successfully execute his agenda and still meet his six o'clock flight back to Houston.

"Marler, I mean Mac? What additional information do you need from me? I met with Terry Johnson and he seemed happy with our financial package. You asked me to come to Chicago to meet with you preferring a face-to-face meeting on the phone. What do you want?" Peter asked in desperation. "I'm here to talk."

McAdams' chuckled and leaned back in his chair. "I don't want anything Peter, much less anything from you," McAdams stated firmly. "I wanted you here in Chicago so I could tell you to your face that I'm taking over your company."

"What!" Peter nearly screamed as he stood and leaned forward placing his hands on the cold glass surface of McAdams' large desk. "You can't take over my company, you only hold a lien on the assets," Peter said in a huff. "What game are you playing here?"

"I assure you son that this is no game," McAdams emphasized without any inflection in his voice. He rummaged around the few papers scattered across the shiny surface of his desk finally locating the object of his search. It was a neatly typed one-page letter. He perused it briefly then slid it across the desk in Peter's direction. "I'm calling your note. It's due and payable in full."

"You can't call my note and demand payment in full without formal notice. Who do you think you are dealing with? I'm not some piker that just fell off the Mardi Gras float from Louisiana!" Peter screamed. "I have rights!"

"After reviewing Union Bank's loan files, we discovered that they have been sending you letters for the past several months notifying TMS that it was out of compliance with the several critical terms of the governing loan agreement. And as to formal notice, I just handed it to you," McAdams stated with great confidence. "My lawyers have blessed everything. You are dead in the water and I hold all of the cards."

"I don't know what you are talking about! My loan is current!" Peter growled. "And even if we are out of compliance, you have to give us a time to cure any defaults before you take any action."

"I thought a man like you would have a better handle on a default situation on your bank loan. Maybe you better check with your CFO."

"I plan to do that as soon as I leave here. In the meantime, I'm working to move my loan to another institution."

"You better move fast," McAdams' warned as he slid a second paper across the desk."

Peter snatched it and quickly read the document. "What is this?" he demanded. "My lawyer will need to review this document."

"Your whore can do whatever she wants. In the meantime we have scheduled a public auction and sale of your company's assets at five o'clock this Friday to pay off the TMS note that I own. I hope for your sake that your new bank can close quickly. Otherwise, by the close of business on Friday afternoon, you will be sitting on the curb and I will own TMS outright."

"Who are you calling a whore?" Peter demanded.

"I understand you two have quite a relationship," McAdams sneered.

"Listen you SOB…"

McAdams held his hand up to stop Peter. "I'm closing you down at the end of the week."

"I need more time," Peter demanded. "You can't expect me to get a new twenty-two million dollar bank deal closed by Friday. You have to be reasonable."

"I don't expect you to get a deal closed. I expect you to fold and walk away. Make it easy on me son," McAdams laughed. "You got two days to pay me off in full. That's it. I will not give you a second longer."

Peter unleashed his anger. He again stood and this time pounded loudly on McAdams' desk nearly shattering the plate glass covering the surface of the desk. In a heavy roar he attacked McAdams. "Listen you son of a bitch! I need a couple of weeks to pull something together with a new bank. I'll even pay you a delay premium to call off the foreclosure auction. A week is all I'm asking."

"You can't have it. You got two days. Come five o'clock Friday, the gavel will come down on your company for good!" McAdams reiterated in a steely cold voice.

"If you sell everything on the auction block, you will get a fraction of its value. The assets are worth nearly one and a half times the debt. Venture Funding is significantly over-secured on the loan," Peter complained. "You don't need to take such drastic action. I personally guarantee payment in full."

McAdams shot back. "Your personal guarantee is worthless!"

"The company's assets are worth a mint."

"That's why these deals are so attractive to Venture Funding and my investors. The profit potential is enormous."

"I'll put the company in a bankruptcy proceeding. That'll stop you dead in your tracks," Peter threatened. "Don't underestimate me."

"If you put this matter in a proceeding, there won't be anything left to fight over. You will certainly destroy whatever value is there. At the end of the day, I'll still have the assets and you will still be on the street. You're too smart to try a chapter proceeding."

"So where do I go from here?" Peter asked.

"I would have thought that a smart man like you would have already figured that one out."

Suddenly Peter realized that his only ally was time and it was rapidly slipping away second by second. The totality of McAdams' plan was now revealed to Peter. The trip to Chicago was a mere delaying tactic. The clock was ticking with Friday heading his direction like a hurricane heading for landfall. There was almost no time remaining to batten down the hatches.

McAdams' laughed with a sinister sneer. "Son, you need to recognize when you've been dry-fucked. You didn't even have time to buy Vaseline. It's all over but the crying. Worst of all, last night you passed on the best whore in Chicago. I know because I've had her many times myself. Go back to Houston and remove your personal stuff from my office," McAdams ordered with a slight snicker.

"What do you expect me to do?" Peter wailed as he once again pounded on McAdams' desk.

"Why Peter Ferrell, I expect you to do nothing."

Peter turned and walked out of McAdams' office. At the receptionist's desk, he barked his orders. "Call me a cab so I can make my flight back to Houston."

"I'm so sorry Mr. Ferrell but I moved your flight back to the late flight because I though you and Mr. McAdams would meet for several more hours. I don't think I can get you back on the six o'clock and the seven o'clock flight is now fully booked."

"So what flight am I on?" Peter asked without trying to hold back his frustration at the turn of events.

"I put you on the eleven o'clock."

"What?" Peter screamed. "That doesn't work at all. I have a thousand things to do between now and Friday. I need to return to Houston immediately."

"That's most unfortunate. It looks like you will not arrive until well after two in the morning."

Peter was furious. McAdams' tactics worked perfectly and Peter fell into his trap far too easily. Then he remembered that it was Megan's idea that he travel to Chicago to meet with McAdams. She was the one who really pushed him into making the trip to Chicago. If he had stayed in Houston, maybe he would be well on the road to blocking McAdams' frontal assault. Without another word, Peter exited Venture Funding's offices to catch a cab to the airport. If Maggie was right and he was unable to change his flight to Houston, then he would spend several unproductive hours at the airport wasting away precious time, time needed to remove the threat McAdams represented.

***

"Peter Ferrell is on his way back to Houston, madder than a hornet," the caller advised. "I'm not sure what direction he will take. You were right when you indicated he was an unpredictable hothead. He can go in any direction. Let's pray that he unwittingly moves straight into our trap."

"Do you think he will throw in the towel and walk away?"

"Not on your life. He's many things but I can guarantee that he is not a quitter."

"What is the next step?"

"Commence phase two."

"Consider it done."

CHAPTER 7

"Truck fueling," the overworked customer service representative answered with her voice straining to remain pleasant. "How may I serve you?"

"This is Union Bank in Houston, Texas. I'm contacting you with some very important information regarding one of our common customers," the caller advised. "This company is very large and if you don't act immediately, you will likely suffer a significant loss."

"What information do you have to share with us today?"

"Earlier, I demanded payment on one of my customers and I understand that you also provide credit to enable them to fuel their fleet of over-the-road trucks. Our bank plans to foreclose on all of the customer's assets after the close of business this Friday. There will be an auction of the company's assets to pay its debt to the bank. Any money that is owed to your organization at that time will not be paid."

"Who is your customer?" the phone representative asked. "I can bring their account up in the system to check our current exposure."

"Union Bank's customer is Transportation Management Services or TMS for short. They are headquartered here in Houston, Texas on Breen Road."

"Here they are. Their payment record is perfect having never missed a single payment. I see that we have considerable credit outstanding. Do you now if they will have any remaining cash to pay to their unsecured creditors?"

"These guys are dead broke. My suggestion is for you to cover your ass as quickly as possible and suspend their fueling privileges immediately."

"I have already e-mailed the information to my manager and he has instructed me to suspend their fueling cards. I can't tell you how much we appreciate the call."

"As one creditor to another, I thought you would like to know sooner rather than later. As creditors we need to stick together and extend every professional courtesy."

※※※

"Taxi!" Peter shouted as he stepped onto the sidewalk outside Venture Funding's offices. He was surprised when a cab immediately pulled out from traffic and up to the curb. Peter opened the door to the rear seat and jumped inside. "O'Hare," he ordered.

The cabbie pulled into traffic and within minutes was traveling west on Interstate 90 headed for the main Chicago airport. Peter quickly rewound the events of the day then replayed in his mind the discussions with both Terry Johnson and Marler McAdams. Within a few miles of Venture's offices, Peter was identifying the individual pieces of his overall strategy to deal with this sudden and very unexpected development. The sooner all of the pieces of the puzzle were fit tightly together the better. Time, what little remained, was absolutely critical. McAdams' nasty reputation as a shrewd and savvy investor was accurate if not somewhat understated. It was incumbent on both Peter and Megan to get down and dirty to win this battle. It was clear that McAdams was a seasoned street fighter who displayed no moral character whatsoever.

Peter reached down and removed his cell phone from its belt clip. He flipped open the cover and scanned the readings. While the system indicated a cell tower within range, the battery reserve was down to a single bar. At best he could make only one telephone call. He couldn't decide whether to call Megan or Woody. If he managed his remaining time judiciously, he just might be able to squeeze a brief call into both. Once at the airport he knew his options increased. He could charge his cell phone or use a public phone. Peter moved through his phone directory until he reached the first party he decided to call. He depressed the call button.

"This is Megan Cedars."

"Megan," Peter said in a reserved tone. "I'm on my way to the airport here in Chicago."

"Is something wrong?" she asked. "Have you finished meeting with McAdams so soon?"

"That son of a bitch is foreclosing on all of the assets of TMS on Friday. He gave me a demand letter. Says the bank has been sending violation notices to Woody for months about a default under the loan agreement and they want to move judiciously to liquidate the assets of the company to pay off the balance on the loan."

"Can you fax the demand letter to me?"

Peter's phone beeped signaling its battery was about to expire. Peter stepped up his pace. "Listen carefully, my phone is about to die. I'm in a cab heading to the airport and will call you from there. Please call Woody and tell him the news." Before Peter could give Megan further instructions, his phone died. He slammed the cover closed and reattached the phone to his belt. Under his breath, he cut loose with a muted scream. Nothing it seemed was going to break in his direction.

At the airport, Peter was able to move up his reservations on a different carrier who would get him home by eleven o'clock. He found a public phone near his departure gate and again called Megan. "I'm on a land line so let me bring you up to date."

"Don't bother," Megan replied. "I think I found something that will help us. If I'm correct, it will give us options."

"Let's discuss your findings when I arrive back in Houston. Can you meet with Woody and me at the office at around eleven thirty?"

"I can meet with you, but I think we need to be careful what we disclose to Woody."

"What in god's name are you suggesting?" Peter demanded his temper starting to uncork. The day was not kind to Peter and his stress level was negatively impacting his already limited control over his fiery temper. "Woody is the most loyal employee I have."

In response to Peter's change in temperament, Megan's demeanor shifted with significantly more edge showing. "Given the developments today, I believe we need to operate with an abundance of caution. We know Deutsch is dirty and didn't you say earlier that the bank has been sending letters to Woody advising him that TMS was in violation of certain loan covenants? Until I have more information we should tread lightly and play our cards close to the vest."

"You think Woody is in on the scam?" Peter asked with his anger simmering just below the surface.

"Maybe he just underestimated the importance of the letters. Banks send all kinds of worthless letters. At times it is difficult to decide which ones are important. But if he is in on the deal, do you want to tell him everything?"

There was a pause in the couple's conversation as each digested the others' recommendation. Peter broke the silence first. "You're right," Peter replied. "Why don't you call him and advise him of the meeting at the terminal. I won't call him and let him remain in the dark. While I wait for my flight, I will charge my phone here at the airport and call you when I arrive in Houston. Then you can head out to the terminal for the meeting. Afterwards, we can go to my house to map out strategy."

On his walk to the gate, Peter stopped by the newsstand to buy a paper. Near the departure gate, he located an electrical outlet, plugged in his cell phone charger and slid his phone under his chair away from traffic. He opened the *USA Today* and settled back in a hard airport seat.

The human traffic at O'Hare was unbelievably heavy as travelers ran to meet their connections. The constant chatter of the gate agents calling flights over the public address system only grated on Peter's already frayed nerves. As he changed sections of the paper, he noticed someone approaching out of the corner of his eye.

"Peter Ferrell?" the stranger asked bending slightly to get a good look at his face. Peter looked up from his paper as the stranger continued. "Yes, I though that was you," the stranger observed as he thrust out his hand to greet Peter. "I'm Joe Campbell from Union Bank. I know we've met several times before. You probably don't remember me, but I knew you father for years. I apologize I never got to know you better."

Peter did not immediately embrace Campbell's invitation. He stared coldly for a few seconds. "You're Jeff Deutsch's boss aren't you?" Peter inquired as he slowly folded the paper and placed it on his lap.

"That is correct," Campbell replied as his smile expanded across his face extending nearly from ear to ear. "You are the last person I expected to run into here in Chicago."

"After all that has happened to me today, I'm not the least bit surprised to see you here. I assume you're here in Chicago to talk to Marler McAdams at Venture Funding about selling more of your good customers down the river," Peter said abruptly as he reopened the paper and continued reading.

"What are you talking about Peter? Who is Marler McAdams?" Campbell asked openly displaying confusion over Peter's biting remarks. "I'm here for a meeting with one of our large correspondent banks."

"Are you trying to tell me you don't know anything about what's going on?"

"I don't have a clue about what you're talking about," Campbell replied. "May I sit?"

Peter put down his paper a second time and looked closely at Campbell's expression. He realized that the banker was sincere and possibly didn't know about the sale of the TMS note. So Peter decided to bring him up to speed. "Two days ago, Union Bank sold my company's note to Marler McAdams of Venture Funding located here in Chicago. Venture Funding is a third rate investor who buys into deals to liquidate companies. I just finished spending to day with his staff only to learn that they are foreclosing on my company after the close of business on Friday."

"What are you talking about? Sold your note! Your company's business is some of the most profitable at the bank. If we would ever consider selling a note and we certainly would never sell to someone who wants to liquidate the collateral assets."

"So you are telling me that the sale was not pushed by bank management as Jeff Deutsch claimed?"

"Absolutely not!"

"All I know is what Jeff Deutsch told me. He said that management at the bank was concerned about the risk in our deal and wanted us out of the bank."

"That's a load of crap. TMS is one of our best customers and we have always seen the credit risk as minimal," Campbell assured Peter. "I told those jug heads in personnel not to hire Deutsch. I understood he was linked to some big problems in Cleveland a couple of years ago. I believe McAdams or someone like him may have been involved. I promise you that I will get this all sorted out tomorrow, and that includes Deutsch."

"I'm really glad I bumped into you Joe. I was in a complete panic. I apologize for my earlier rudeness."

"Don't worry. This will all be back to normal tomorrow. I will call you first thing in the morning. If Deutsch sold your note without my knowledge, you have every right to be upset."

The Boeing 757 touched down at Bush Intercontinental Airport at exactly eleven o'clock. Peter grabbed his duffle bag and exited the plane. His cell fully charged and he called Megan. "I got some great news," he reported. "I met Joe Campbell from Union Bank at O'Hare. He says that bank management never authorized the sale of our note. He will get on it first thing in the morning. So we can stop working to move the loan."

"That is great news. However, given McAdams' reputation, I think we need to continue with a parallel plan until our paper is back in the bank. I spoke to Woody and he will meet us at the terminal at eleven thirty. I'm on the Hardy Toll Road now and should be in your office in about five minutes. Have you thought any more about Woody's possible involvement?" Megan asked.

"I want to believe he wouldn't do anything to harm the company. Unfortunately, after meeting McAdams combined with what I have learned about Deutsch, anything is possible. It would certainly not be beyond someone like Marler McAdams to bribe a company officer for information or cooperation. Is there a way we can smoke Woody out?" Peter inquired.

"Let me think about it. Again please be careful what you say to him during our meeting."

When Peter arrived at TMS, he found Megan in his office on the phone. He walked to Woody's office and pulled up a chair. Woody looked up and spoke first. "I understand the meeting in Chicago didn't go well."

"That's an understatement. I went awful. But how did you know about my meeting with Marler McAdams?" Peter asked hesitantly.

Without looking up from his work, Woody replied, "Megan told me when she called me earlier."

"Have you spoken to the other banks today?" Peter asked without hesitation. "Where do they stand? Is there any way they can speed up a closing?"

"I spoke to both today and neither can do anything for a week, maybe two," Woody reported.

"Damn!" Peter cursed. "I need them to step up and help us out of this predicament"

"That's not the worst of it," Woody said. "Our trucks can't fuel."

"What are you talking about?" Peter demanded. "We have never had a single problem with our fleet card provider."

"They cut off our credit cold this morning. Said they got a report that we are having financial problems. They want cash up front to prepay what we expect to use. Not only that but they demanded we immediately wire them full payment of all outstanding fueling receipts, about a quarter of a million dollars."

"Who could have told them we were having financial problems?" Peter cried. "Shit, can anything go my way today?"

"My money is on McAdams," Woody surmised. "He's working overtime to disrupt our business."

"I agree with your assessment. It's McAdams who is pulling the strings. So what are you doing about it?" Peter demanded. "How do we neutralize this guy?"

"First, I sent the fuel provider the payment they requested and a little extra to pre-pay a week's worth of fueling. I've also contacted several of the big truck stops we use and they say they will let some of our trucks fuel to get their deliveries made but that's it. Tomorrow, I will give all of our drivers enough cash to fill-up several times. For other suppliers, I will call the bank and wire money to pre-pay for fuel. That should keep everything rolling along smoothly."

"It is now clear that this is all part of McAdams' master plan. The more fires he creates for us to fight, the fewer resources we have at our disposal to fight him."

"It certainly fits his reputation," Woody observed. "So tell me, what the heck happened in Chicago?"

Before Peter could relate the sequence of events from Chicago, Megan walked into the room. "Where do we stand?" Peter asked. "Time is running out."

"I think we need to start to consider alternative strategies." Megan reported. "I'm still working on the documents but it is looking like we will only have a small window of opportunity in which to operate. We need to think about a white knight."

"A white knight, are you insane?" Peter asked. "I don't want to lose control of the company. We have other banks looking at this deal and Campbell is at the front of the pack to help us resolve this matter."

The two men sensed anger building inside Megan. She stepped back a few steps and exhaled heavily. "McAdams is planning to foreclose on Friday. We need as many irons in the fire as we can get. You are never going to get to next week. You have two days, that's it!"

"Foreclose!" Woody gasped. "What do you mean foreclose?"

Peter leaned forward. "McAdams told me that we are in default of certain covenants in our loan agreement with the bank. He has demanded payment in full."

"He has to first tell us we are out of compliance and give us time to cure," Woody interjected.

"Interesting that you mention that," Peter replied coldly. "McAdams gave me copies of letters the bank sent to you over the past many months telling you that we were out of compliance. As the new owner of the note, he is building on those notices and has demanded payment by Friday. If we don't pay in full, he has scheduled a public auction for five o'clock. Is there something you need to tell us?"

Woody was silent. He lowered his head and stared at the clutter on the surface of his desk. His silence did not improve the demeanor of TMS' attorney. Megan released a verbal assault. "What in the fuck is going on here Woody? Where are the letters and why haven't you told us of their existence?" she demanded. "How many times have I told you to copy me on all correspondence from Union Bank?"

Woody swung his head from side to side. "They didn't seem important at the time. After I started getting the letters from the bank, I called Deutsch and he told me they were only a formality and that I should ignore them. The bank merely sent them to keep the banking regulators happy, file documentation kind of shit. It all seemed so innocent."

Megan questioned Woody further. "What did you mean when you said after the letters started?"

"TMS has been out of compliance under the terms of Union Bank's loan agreement for about a year now. Crap, we have been out of compliance in one area or another ever since we signed the renewal agreement two years ago. The bank never did anything in the past. Then about six months ago, the letters started showing up."

"Well, that's a fine pickle you've gotten us into," Peter cursed.

Megan interjected. "McAdams has been planning this for months. The letters never came before because the bank didn't care. McAdams had Deutsch send the letters laying the framework for your meeting today. He has a massive head start. We have to believe he knows our next move because he is controlling the strings and he thinks we don't know."

"Regardless, Woody should have told us," Peter said. "You let me down!"

"Okay I screwed up!" Woody shouted in an attempt to defuse the situation. "I know that to say I'm sorry isn't going to fix the problem," Woody offered sounding genuinely concerned over his inaction. "You said you need other options like a white knight. Well, call Phil Elmore."

Megan spoke up. "Who is Phil Elmore?"

"He owns Dallas Metro Trucking. Several years ago, Peter's father talked to Phil about a possible merger. I think the only reason it didn't go through was because at the end of the day Peter's dad wanted to keep TMS family-owned so one day it would be yours," Woody said turning to Peter. "I'll bet he can move quickly on a deal. He is flush with cash and has always wanted to expand into our markets. I know he would welcome a call from you."

"I don't remember Dad ever saying anything about a merger. I always thought that giving up any control of the company was the last thing he wanted."

"Peter, your dad didn't tell you everything. I think he was unsure whether you really wanted to make this company your life. Your dad knew he didn't have a choice about taking over the business. He wanted you to have the choice, but he just died too soon."

Megan looked at Peter. "It's worth a shot. With a viable alternative in hand, we can better bargain with McAdams."

"I will call him first thing in the morning and see if I can fly up to see him."

"Then let's call it a day. The next two days are certain to keep us on our toes," Woody said.

The meeting adjourned with Peter and Megan returning to Peter's office to continue with their conversation. In the quietness of the office they waited until Woody left the building. Megan moved to the door and peered into the hall. She turned and whispered to Peter, "I want to make sure Woody is gone." She stepped out of Peter's office and walked to the window in the reception area. She peered outside and saw that Woody's parking place was empty. She returned to Peter's office, closed the door to the office and collapsed into one of the chairs.

Megan then disclosed to Peter her preliminary findings. "At the renewal of your bank loan four years ago, it appears that the attorney handling the documents made a serious error. The error was carried forward when the loan was last renewed two years ago. The security documents are incomplete. And that error may leave the door open for us to stop McAdams dead in his tracks."

"I don't understand," Peter said. "How can the documents be wrong?"

"Banks renew loans repeatedly over many years. With each renewal, they generally reuse the same asset schedules rather than retyping them. The practice saves costs and time. No one cares or checks for accuracy since few loans eventually go into default where foreclosure is required. It is only within the context of a foreclosure action that absolute accuracy is required. Recycling asset schedules represents a minimal risk which most banks are willing to accept."

"How can the documents be incorrect," Peter asked in confusion. "It makes no sense to me. How were accurate at one time and then they weren't?"

Megan smiled at Peter's obvious confusion. To help him comprehend the complexity of the situation, she detailed the exact nature of the error in the collateral documents supporting the TMS loan. "Let me make this as basic as possible. When TMS originally borrowed from Union Bank about ten years ago, it pledged all of the company's assets behind the loan. The attorney drawing up the security documents typed a schedule individually listing each asset. In the case of TMS, this required several legal pages. To be more exact, it required three complete pages and about four lines on a fourth page. At a renewal about four years ago, somehow the fourth page was omitted. I guess that since it was mostly blank, the paralegal assembling the closing package thought it was completely blank. The loan documents were appropriately signed at the closing with the security documents filed at the county. Since the fourth page was omitted those assets listed on the page were not included in the pledge or for that matter the filing. At the last renewal two years ago, the error was not caught and again those assets were omitted from the security documents. Therefore they are free and clear of any liens. When Venture Funding forecloses on Friday, they won't be selling those assets."

"The error is so minor, how can it be important?" Peter asked.

"There is no question that the error is minor, but under the law, accuracy rules and the assets are clearly not pledged. And while the error is minor, the assets involved are significant."

Peter thought for a moment then challenged Megan's assertions. "I don't question the accuracy of your analysis, but how did McAdams' attorney miss such a glaring error? I wouldn't think he misses anything."

"The error is so slight I almost missed it myself. I was reviewing Leslie's work and noticed the discrepancy. She also missed it in the initial review. And remember, McAdams assumed that the bank's documents were complete."

"Refresh my memory. Who is Leslie?" Peter inquired.

"Leslie Goodwin is my paralegal. Maybe I haven't mentioned her before," Megan acknowledged. "She has only been with me for about six months. I assigned her the task to look over the loan documents. Since she is still in training I decided to review her work. When I first brought the error to her attention, she tried to argue that I was wrong. She stated that documentation attorneys just don't make such glaring mistakes. But when I showed her what I found, she admitted that she was wrong."

"So I'm home free," Peter nearly shouted. "Tomorrow I'm calling Marler McAdams and tell him where he can stick his foreclosure sale up his ass!"

Megan held up her hand. "Not so fast. This won't stop the foreclosure completely. It just gives us another option to get you out of this mess with some money in your pocket. The note sale by Union Bank is still valid and the default remains uncured. McAdams remains in the driver's seat. Now, it appears he holds only half your ass, not the whole thing."

If Megan possessed any consistent trait, it was caution. Her slow deliberate style saved TMS from losses on many occasions. Early in their relationship, Peter learned not to argue with Megan when she was at the helm. Her instincts were unimpeachable. Once Peter referred to her as a fine thoroughbred who required only modest levels of attention and recognition to maintain her peak performance.

Peter laughed slightly at Megan's remarks. He knew better than to laugh openly. She pulled the massive chair close to the desk and opened her briefcase. "Do you think it is possible that Woody is working for McAdams?" Peter asked. "It all seems circumstantial. Maybe we are just seeing bad guys behind every tree. You heard him tonight. He is working as hard as he can to help get us out of this bind."

Megan huffed loudly, "Maybe too hard."

"What does that mean?" Peter demanded.

"Hold the tude!" Megan instructed. "I'm not accusing him of anything. Right now all I know is that it's damn late and I'm tired as worn out washrag. Right now, we are the only two people I trust, and I'm not sure why I even trust you. You have a full day tomorrow, so let me get out of here."

"Before we separate, Joe Campbell said something about Deutsch being involved in some deal gone bad in Cleveland before he came to Houston. He also thinks McAdams might have been involved. It would be great if we could get some details on what happened. I don't know...maybe it could help us here."

"I agree," Megan responded. "I'll get my investigator on it tomorrow."

"I thought we could go to my house and talk about us. I've done plenty of thinking and..."

"Not tonight," Megan said softly. She moved near and handed Peter a synopsis of her findings. "Look this over and we can talk tomorrow." She leaned forward and kissed Peter on the cheek. "Sometimes it takes a jolt to the system before you can see clearly. In a couple of weeks we will look back on this time and laugh."

"I like hearing that we will be still talking in several weeks."

"Make a list of what you need to do the next forty-eight hours. And don't forget that you need to call your both mother and uncle, and advise them of the situation."

"Shit I forgot all about Valerie and Stuart. You're right. I will call both of them tomorrow morning."

Megan picked up her purse and walked out of Peter's office. In a few seconds he heard the main door to the office close followed shortly by the sound of her car speeding east down Breen Road.

Peter sat quietly at his desk jotting down the list of must do items as Megan instructed. His concentration was broken when his phone rang. He looked at the caller ID and saw that it was Woody Coppell.

Peter picked up the phone but before he could say a word Woody started talking. "We can't lose control of TMS. There has been too much blood spilled by so many people over the years. We'll win this fight because the good guys win at the end of the day," Woody told Peter in a reassuring tone.

"The A team is on the trail and I am certain that we will make it out alive. Bastards like McAdams don't always win," Peter sighed.

"Has Megan found anything?" Woody asked. "She is so damn competent that I thought surely she would ferret out that rabbit in the hat."

Peter paused before answering. After a few seconds, he blurted, "Megan thinks she has found some errors in the Union Bank loan documents."

"What kind of errors?" Woody asked with excitement in his voice. "Any news is good news."

Once again Peter found himself in a deep hole of his own creation. Megan specifically told him not to reveal any of her findings to Woody, but like so many times before, he didn't think before pulling the trigger on his mouth. This time Peter quickly stepped back and regrouped. "I don't know. She hasn't given me the details yet."

"Will it save the company from foreclosure?"

"I don't know for certain," Peter disclosed. "These legal details can confound a Rhode scholar."

"Well this is wonderful news. Now it is starting to look like we can rest easier. Do you want to meet me for a drink to celebrate?" Woody asked. "It's been a long time since we did anything like that."

"I just want to go home and get some sleep. It has been an extremely long day," Peter told Woody.

Peter hung up the phone, picked up the notepad with his pending items list and reclined in his chair. Outside he heard the steady drone of large over-the-road rigs moving continuously into and out of the terminal. As a youth he found the activity exciting. Tonight, he was overcome by a shroud of ambivalence. The stress and tension were becoming unbearable. A voice inside his head screamed for him to stand up and run out of the building, get in his truck and drive away. But then that was the easy way out. Peter was no longer the carefree teenager who freely roamed the terminal years ago. He tossed the list on his desk and exited the building. Nothing more could be accomplished at this hour.

CHAPTER 8

"It's late. This better be important."

"There's an error in the bank documents. That bitch Cedars thinks she has something."

"Impossible! They have been checked and rechecked."

"I don't care what level of due diligence has occurred. I'm telling you they have discovered several errors in the documents. They may be significant enough to stop the auction sale on Friday."

"What is the nature of the errors?"

"I don't know. They were tight lipped with the details."

"Then find out and call me back as soon as you learn anything concrete."

***

At home in Bellaire, Peter climbed down from his massive vehicle. The demands of the past several days wore heavy. He was more tired and exhausted than he could remember. A hot shower and some rest would recharge his batteries. His mind raced nonstop as he tried his best to bring order and sanity to what was happening. None of it added up. The sequence of events moved so quickly that it was clear Peter and TMS were victims of a well-choreographed dance with no missteps to date by the opposition. Megan was spot on in her conclusions that Marler McAdams had worked behind the scenes on this takeover action for months. To this point his execution was flawless.

Once in the house, Peter retrieved a cold Budweiser from the refrigerator and grabbed a large bag of potato chips from the counter. He popped the top on the beer, tore open the bag of chips and fell back into his leather Laz-a-Boy rocker recliner. He reached into the open bag, grabbed a handful of chips and shoved several in his mouth. Slowly his functions returned to normal. The clock in the kitchen struck two. In less than two days the foreclosure auction would permanently close out his family's business and he felt as though he was no closer to a solution than when he first got the call from Deutsch.

Peter picked up the phone from the lamp table and called Megan. She answered immediately. "I knew you would call," she confessed. Her tone was calm and relaxed. "I can't go to sleep. This matter has me all discombobulated."

"I had to call. I wanted to hear your voice."

"I like hearing you say that," Megan purred softly. "What's on your mind?"

"I can't stop thinking about what you said about Woody possibly working for the opposition. I'm starting to get a sick feeling that he's on the take. The fact that he did nothing with those blasted notices sticks in my craw. Without those damn notices, there is no threat of immediate foreclosure. I can't get that fact out of my head."

"Now you are sounding like me," Megan laughed.

"That's because we think alike."

"We are both highly suspicious of others," Megan said in agreement. "Is there anything else?"

"After you left the terminal tonight, Woody called and rattled on and on that we have to save TMS. It was so out of character for him. He even asked if I wanted to get a drink and commiserate."

"The more I've thought about it the more I'm of the opinion that Woody is just lazy. He ignored the letters rather than dealing with them. You have said yourself many times that he just doesn't get stuff done around the office," Megan concluded. "After all, he's a senior level long term employee. I wouldn't expect him to turn on his employer."

"And as far as an employee doing something like this, at TMS we find long-term employees stealing from us all of the time. They steal from the terminal. They steal off the trucks. They steal fuel. If it isn't fucking nailed down, it's history. I will never understand why they do it."

"I guess they have many reasons," Megan offered.

"Their reasons don't matter. To get the work done, I have no choice but to place people in positions of responsibility where the only thing I have is the blind trust that they will do the right thing at the end of the day. There is nothing else I can do. I know I'm over reacting but shit, I never thought I would get screwed by someone so close."

"It is always those closest to you who hurt you the most," Megan responded softly.

Megan's words hit her intended mark. Her few simple words knocked Peter for a loop. He remained speechless. He took a few moments to fully digest Megan's last comments. With a heavy sigh he responded, "I get your point. I'll drop it."

"There is nothing for you to drop. I'm a trained corporate attorney. It is not in my nature to suspect people of wrongdoing. I walk into every business meeting believing in the total honesty of all the participants. If I questioned everyone's morals, I couldn't get my job done."

"If only I could do the same. But I can't," Peter stated firmly. "It isn't my nature."

In an accommodating tone, Megan softly sighed, "That's why we compliment one another."

Peter replied calmly, "That's the way I have always seen our relationship. And I am so sorry for the way I acted the other night."

The phone conversation fell silent for almost thirty seconds, with neither responding to the other's remarks. They both were unsure what they should say next. Finally, Megan decided to break the uncomfortable silence. "But if you do suspect Woody is dirty, then it is best we not tell him anything about our intentions for dealing with this matter. Frankly, I don't see how he can help us out of this predicament either way."

"Fuck!"

"What is it?" Megan asked. "What did I say?"

"I told the bastard about your findings on the documents."

Megan raised her voice in response to Peter's untimely disclosure. "Exactly how much did you tell him about the error I found?" Megan asked.

"I told Woody that you found an error in the documents. Nothing more."

"Did he act surprised or probe for more detail?"

"Aren't you going to scream at me for doing something so stupid?"

Megan ignored Peter's offer for a scolding. She repeated her question. "How much did you tell him?"

"I couldn't tell him many of the facts since I don't fully understand the issue myself," Peter confessed. "I disclosed only the basics that there was an error in the documents but you weren't sure how it could be used."

Megan thought about Peter's revelation for a few minutes. "This may actually be good in the long run."

"If he is working with Venture Funding, our strategy may well be wrecked."

"Not necessarily. Here is how I see it. We're unsure whether Woody is working with McAdams and earlier I asked you what could we do to smoke Woody out from the shadows?"

Peter spoke up. "That is assuming he is hiding in the shadows for McAdams."

"What specifically is he supposedly working on which you can independently verify? Maybe that way you can check on his activities without revealing your cards."

"I can't think of anything."

"There has to be something. My god, what does this man do for the company?" Megan asked tersely.

"Since this whole disaster started, he's been talking to other banks in town about taking over our banking relationship. I didn't see it as a viable option once McAdams called the loan. The banks simply can't move fast enough to save the company."

Megan did not immediately respond.

"Did you hear what I said?" Peter asked. "He's been working on moving our banking relationship. I haven't questioned him on the matter because, well, to be honest, it just fell off my radar screen."

Megan's silence angered Peter. "Do you think I dropped the ball?" Peter demanded.

"Calm down. I heard you and no I don't think that you dropped the ball. I agree that the banks can't move quickly enough to save the company from foreclosure. If there is going to be win here for the home team, you and I are the only ones that can put the checkmark in the win column."

"So I have been wasting my time with the whole bank strategy?" Peter concluded with frustration in his voice.

"You have not been wasting your time. McAdams must think that you are running around in total desperation trying to save the company. If he thinks you are running in a circle, he will drop his guard. That may be just the opening we need."

"Then I am back to the original question. Is Woody dirty?" Peter asked.

"I was trying to think of a reason that would tempt Woody to team up with the opposition."

"You want a reason, try money!" Peter shouted. "The right amount of money will corrupt anyone, regardless of their loyalty or morality. It's the most basic mathematical formula."

"It's biblical if nothing else," Megan responded. "But if I remember correctly, isn't Woody the second highest paid employee in the company behind you. How much money can Marler wave in his face to bring him over to his side?"

"Are you saying you now think he's dirty?"

"I'll withhold judgment for now. But if McAdams does have a mole in the company, then his actions would be calculated to put you off his trail?" Megan suggested. "Send the wolf down a box canyon. That is exactly what a bastard like Marler McAdams would do in this situation. Look at the sequence of events since Deutsch called. You have been spinning your wheels while the hours ticked away."

"I don't want to over analyze this, but it would seem like the right thing to do if you are trying to cover all of the bases. I will call tomorrow and check on the status of the bank requests. That way he won't know what I am doing. I will find out whether he actually did what I asked."

"That's a great idea!" Megan exclaimed. "Then we will be in the driver's seat for a change."

"That's where I want to be, steering this fucking train wreck!"

"Then it's agreed. You will call the banks tomorrow."

"If Woody did his job, they should be on the cusp of a decision. If not then we know for certain that he is in bed with McAdams."

"I know I will feel much better knowing whose team he is on."

"If he hasn't followed up with the banks, I will immediately fire his ass."

"Wait a minute Peter!" Megan cautioned. "If he is dirty, the last thing we want to do is let him know that we are on to him. We may be able to turn a little knowledge to our advantage."

"How can it be to our benefit to have a snitch in our ranks?" Peter asked.

"It will give us the opportunity to feed his friend in Chicago a steady diet of misinformation. Then we can execute our strategy right under his noses."

"I will feel much better if he is on the take. But if he isn't, then we are nowhere."

"And that's exactly where we are standing right now."

"You couldn't be more right," Peter observed. "Something else has been bothering me since I first met with the team at Venture Funding."

"Not tonight. There are already enough twists and turns for me to comprehend. Before this plays out to the bitter end, I'm going to need a score card to keep track of all of the players," Megan stressed. "I'm tired and need to get some sleep. We can talk again in the morning."

"No," Peter interjected. "Don't hang up yet. Just one more thought."

"Okay but make it quick," Megan said her voice for the first time showing signs of stress.

Peter paused for a moment to organize his thoughts before continuing. "Try this one on for size," Peter started. "Maybe Deutsch sent the notice letters to the company to set us up and we really aren't out of compliance. No one has validated the claim that we are in default. We are taking Woody's word that the letters are accurate. Now if he is in on the scam, then he could be lying. With three you've got a conspiracy."

"That's a different angle I hadn't considered. It sounds plausible but I don't know."

"Shouldn't we at least explore it?" Peter asked.

"In the morning you can have Bill Cobb investigate the matter," Megan insisted. "With the auction scheduled to start in less than two days, if TMS is not out of compliance, then we can petition the court to stay the sale. But once the auctioneer starts, it is all over regardless of the status of any violations."

"Maybe there is another option. Since all we owe is what we owe, lets out bid Venture Funding at the auction. That way the note gets paid and we still own TMS."

"That's a good idea, but you will need financing. We can't buy him out without twenty-two million dollars in cash."

"We can get it from Union Bank. When I call Joe Campbell tomorrow, I will ask him for a new loan," Peter offered. "They should be willing to do anything to get out of this messy situation."

Megan again went silent. "Fine, it's another option to explore. Given the screw up here, I think they may want to help. A new bank loan on such short notice may require the assistance of your mother and uncle to encourage the bank to make a move since they own more than half of the company. You can go ahead try presenting your proposal to Campbell, but I think taking the legal angle will work better. What about this Elmore option?"

"I will do what Woody recommends and call Elmore tomorrow morning."

"Can you trust this guy Elmore? Maybe this is a rouse and nothing more," Megan speculated. "It could well be another box canyon."

"You may be correct. I can check it out before I make any firm commitments. This should also help confirm our suspicions about Woody."

"If we can't get this option moving forward and we end up at the auction, do you think your mother and uncle would be willing to come into a refinance deal with their financial support?"

"You know how my mom feels about the company. She is iffy at best. And as for Uncle Stuart, he checked out of the company years ago and is in a happy place."

Megan agreed. "It was worth a try."

"I will meet with them tomorrow and report to them what is happening. But don't hold your breath."

Megan moved to cut off further conversation. "Let me repeat. It is late. We need to end this endless discussion and get some rest."

Peter agreed and wrapped up on his end. "I've enjoyed taking to you Megan. In the future I want all of our conversations to be like this one."

"Normal?"

"Yes."

CHAPTER 9

On Thursday morning, Peter awoke abruptly, slowly rolled over and glanced at the alarm clock on the night table. The current time displayed by the large red digital numbers was seven thirty. As if hit by a bolt of lightening, Peter suddenly realized that something was out of kilter. He sat up in his bed and grabbed the clock from the night table. At first he could not understand why the alarm had not sounded. Then he realized to his dismay that the light for the alarm was not illuminated. It hit him immediately. He forgot to turn on the alarm when he retired for the evening. The conversation with Megan drained clear thinking from his head. The habitual motion to set the alarm each evening was so instinctive that he could not recall his failure from the evening before. Rather than lose his temper, he simply bolted from bed and walked briskly into the bathroom.

It was after ten to eight when Peter walked through the office door at TMS. He moved past Heather's desk and walked briskly down the hall to Woody's office. "Any status updates on our loan requests from the banks?" Peter asked as he started to pace in front of Woody's desk. "Time is quickly running out. Something has got to break this damn logjam."

"Didn't set your alarm last night?" Woody asked laughing under his breath. "You're here awfully late. I fully expected to see you here when I arrived at six."

"It's not important. Tell me where do we stand with the banks?" Peter again asked sounding increasingly frustrated.

"Nothing firm from either bank yet. I will call them when they open this morning. It should be good news because the credit analyst that Texas Merchants assigned to do the legwork on our request called yesterday for additional information. She reported that the deal looked excellent and her recommendation should be ready to go out to management by early afternoon yesterday."

"That's great," Peter said as he sat. "Did she give you any indication about when they would have our request approved?"

"She is too junior to have that level of information. I can only assume that they will press forward with utmost speed," Woody advised. "Can you update me on Megan's progress? Does she think she get the foreclosure stopped?"

"There is no news at this juncture but she keeps plugging away. I did forget to tell you that I ran into Joe Campbell in the Chicago airport yesterday."

"Isn't he Deutsch's boss at Union Bank?"

"The one and only," Peter quipped.

"What did he have to say when he saw you? That must have been pretty awkward for him after what they pulled?" Woody suggested. "I'm surprised he even spoke to you. He should have crawled under the nearest jet way and remained out of sight."

"In fact, our meeting was just the opposite. Campbell was quite talkative. It seems clear now that he knew nothing about the sale. When I gave him the lowdown, he nearly went into a rage and has offered to fully investigate the matter when he returns to the bank. He wants the loan repurchased as soon as possible."

"That's wonderful news. Does he think he can get it done by the end of the day tomorrow?"

"It's anyone's guess what those bumbling bankers can get done and when."

"What does Megan advise you to do?" Woody asked as he looked down at his work spread across his desk. "She must have a pretty strong opinion in this matter."

"If she had her way, she would have me pack up my office and walk away. Since she knows I won't do that, her advice is to proceed on all fronts simultaneously. Keep all of the irons hot in the fire."

"I agree with Megan. Spend every remaining minute working as many of the viable angles that you can. That gives you the most flexibility."

"Along the lines of looking at all of the angles, tell me more about this Elmore character. What's his story?"

Woody leaned back in his chair and opened one of the large filing drawers in his desk. As he thumbed through the many files in the drawer, he talked to Peter about this possible white knight. "I can't remember the exact timing," he started. "I guess it was about a year after you arrived at TMS after graduating from Texas. Your father met several times with Phil Elmore about a possible merger. It would have been a great fit. Elmore's company, Dallas Metro Trucking had been around for many years but had never been able to penetrate our core markets. The combination of both companies would have produced significant synergies and tripled profitability with virtually no increase in costs. Between the two companies there was no duplication in customers, equipment or terminals."

"I think I've heard of them, but since we don't directly compete against them, I don't know much about them." Peter revealed.

"They are primarily a hub and spoke operation while we focus on cross country. Our two operations complimented one another perfectly. That's why the merger looked like a great fit. Sort of a marriage made in heaven," Woody insisted.

"So why didn't Dad go through with the deal?" Peter asked. "From what you are saying, the combined company would have created the biggest independent trucking operation in the region."

"Well, like I said, you had just arrived and John wanted to give you the opportunity to eventually run the combined business. Phil isn't much older than you are and like you, inherited a family business. He had no plans of stepping down. In the end I believe that was the final nail in the coffin that killed the deal."

"Personally, I hate the idea of a merger regardless of how perfect it is. Staying independent is the best way to run a business," Peter said. "Bringing in a second ownership group would only have mucked everything up. Don't you want to be our own bosses?"

"Whatever works for you?" Woody replied with some harshness in his tone. "Remember, you're the boss, not me."

"Dad never told me he considered merging or selling out," Peter disclosed.

"I'm happy that the deal didn't go through," Woody revealed.

"Why would you feel that way if it was such a great fit?" Peter asked displaying confusion over Woody's comments to the contrary.

"Elmore runs his staff and equipment hard, too hard in my opinion. He has high employee turnover and his company's accident rate is one of the highest in the industry."

"If it makes money, what's wrong with getting the most out of your asset base?"

"Keeping the lid on tight and constantly keeping the fire burning at maximum creates constant breakdowns and causes needless headaches. I prefer the slower deliberate pace around here. We make plenty of money and the staff works hard for us. The added stress doesn't justify the few extra nickels you accumulate for the bottom line."

"I'm glad to hear that Dad wanted me to have the company," Peter said smoothly as a large smile grew across his face. "You probably don't know, but Dad and I never spoke much. I rarely got the opportunity to see all of his different sides. He could be rather cold around the office as well as at home. This is a wonderful revelation that he wanted me to run the company."

"I didn't say that your dad wanted you to have the business. I said your dad wanted to give you the opportunity to decide for yourself the future of the company. If your interests were not in the trucking business, then that was fine with him."

Peter chided his CFO over his remarks. "Dad loved this business and would have never relinquished control. He fully expected me to hand it down to my son. That much I do know. You don't know what you are talking about."

"Peter let's not get into a fight over this. Yes, John loved this business but recognized that his unflinching devotion ruined his marriage and was probably the biggest single contributing factor to his limited relationship with you. He was unbelievably sad that his total commitment to TMS made your mother miserable and unhappy. When we were going through the due diligence with Dallas Metro, he told me that he really wanted to exit the rat race and patch things up with your mother. His love for you caused him to remain in the company. That's why he rejected the merger offer. Unfortunately, I believe the strain of the business after talks with Dallas Metro broke down ultimately led to his demise. He died within a year after he ended merger discussions with Elmore."

The information was more than Peter could handle given the inordinate amount of stress bearing down on him. Without further conversation he quickly exited Woody's office and walked down the hall. Once inside his office, he closed the door.

Woody realized that the significance of these sudden revelations caught Peter squarely by surprise. He continued his search for the business card for Dallas Metro's owner. When he found it, he walked to Peter's office and tapped lightly on the door. As he eased it open and looked inside he found Peter sitting behind his desk with his chair turned facing the wall. Woody quietly moved toward Peter's desk then placed the card gentle on the corner of the desk.

As he backed away, he spoke softly, "I knew I had the number for Dallas Metro around here somewhere. When you feel like it, give Phil a call."

Before Woody could exit the office, Peter started to speak although he continued to stare at the wall behind his desk. "I don't know whether this merger is the path I want to take. The stress of this deadline tomorrow and now the revelations surrounding all of these family issues are really weighing heavy on me. I may not have any other options, but right now I'm having difficulty cutting loose of the company without a fight."

"All you have to do is call Elmore and see if he has any interest. Maybe he is willing to consider different terms. It's been ten years since he and John last spoke. You don't have to decide anything until after the two of you discuss interests and options. What do you have to lose? He may be your only salvation. I know how difficult it is to suck up your pride. Let me be honest, we would have been better friends long ago if it wasn't for your stupid pride."

Peter spun around and leaned forward in his chair. Woody's candid remarks both surprised and angered him. "I have many faults," he acknowledged. "And you are not the first to point out my weaknesses. If you have something on your mind that you have been holding back, give it to me. If you have nothing, then walk out?"

Woody clearly saw redness in Peter's eyes. For an instant, he considered going easy on his boss but he couldn't hold it in any longer. The years of restraint collapsed. Woody leaned forward and rested his hands on the surface of Peter's desk. "I have nothing more than this. Your ego is far too big for the good of this company. This is a great company, but you didn't build it. Dewey and John did. In your ten years here, all you have done is build your own ego. Fundamentally, this company is unchanged from the one you inherited the day you moved into this office. Shit, your mother and uncle could have put a monkey in here as a caretaker and he would have done no worse than you!" Woody said with venom in his tone. "This business is just a fleet of trucks and a falling down building. All that was left to you was a cash machine nothing more. This is not the legacy that you believe it is."

Peter did not reply. He just sat quietly staring at Woody. With a loud huff, Woody turned and left the office. Peter picked up the business card lying on the corner of his desk and rotated it through his slender fingers. When he stopped, he stared at the information printed on the front of the card. He couldn't decide what to do. He looked at his watch. Time was rapidly running out and the list of options was thinning. Maybe this was the right time to get out of the business permanently. He reached for his phone and quickly tapped in the phone number.

Peter's call was answered at Dallas Metro on the first ring. He asked to speak to Phil Elmore and the receptionist placed him on hold. Within a few minutes, Elmore came on the line. Peter opened the conversation diving directly into his sales pitch. "Phil, this is Peter Ferrell with Transportation Management Services in Houston. I understand you and my father spoke about a merger a number of years ago, so I hope you know who we are."

Elmore cleared his throat then started to speak in a very raspy voice. "If my memory serves me, your father's name was John was it not?"

Peter was impressed with Elmore's recollection of meetings that occurred almost ten years earlier. "Yes, that was my father, John Ferrell. He passed away about eight years ago. I have been running the company since his death."

"I do remember your father as first class gentleman," he offered. "Tell me Peter, what is the purpose of your call?"

Peter hesitated for a moment. He was about to take the most significant step in his life. He drew a heavy breath and pondered the moment. Try as he might, words refused to come out of his mouth for the longest time. Finally, his throat loosened and the words flowed. "Phil, when my father spoke to you, I believe the discussion centered on a potential merger between Dallas Metro and TMS. As the industry has changed in recent years, I have decided that maybe it's the right time to sell the company. I assume a combination of our two companies is still as good a fit now as it was back when you and my father spoke. So, you see the purpose of my call is to explore your interests in purchasing TMS."

"I must say this call is the last thing I expected. Ten years ago, it seemed that we were on the fast lane to a deal when your father suddenly folded his tent and returned to Houston. I was extremely disappointed that the earlier deal fell through. It was a match made in heaven. Our respective organizations compliment one another so perfectly. I have been following your organization since those earlier meetings and was thinking about approaching you again early next year. But if you want to do something now, I guess that works for me."

"Great," Peter replied almost shouting into the phone. "We need to move immediately."

"Hold on Peter. We haven't even discussed price. This is undoubtedly a transaction of significant size. What are you asking?" Elmore asked. "I'm not going to be taken to the cleaners."

"I want thirty million cash," Peter shot back immediately without any hesitation whatsoever. "I do not want to negotiate. It's a very fair price and the company is worth every penny. We both know that." Peter wanted to make sure Dallas Metro was a viable candidate able to come to the closing table with sufficient funds. "Is there a problem raising the money?"

"I currently have much more than thirty million dollars available under my revolving bank line. I have to be honest and tell you that thirty million is a pretty steep price for your company. There is no question that your company has value, but your price is still a little high." After thinking about the offer a few seconds, Elmore responded to Peter's number. "I agree that it's a fair price."

Peter was surprised by Elmore's quick agreement on the price. He was sure he would want to negotiate a much lower price. Maybe Peter threw out too low a number on the table. He should have run it by Woody before calling Elmore. Once again, just like the meeting with Marler McAdams, he thought he could wing it. Woody was right, a trained monkey could do no worse. "I will get my attorney to draw up the sale documents."

"Hold on," Elmore shot back. "I need a few days to consider your offer."

"I can't give you a few days. We need to close immediately, well no later than tomorrow," Peter stressed.

"Are you in some kind of trouble?" Elmore suddenly demanded. "You call up out of the blue offering to sell out, now you say you want the money immediately. That always translates into trouble in my book. Give me the honest to god truth here. Has TMS taken a turn for the worse?"

"My bank here in Houston sold my loan to a private investor who is now pressing me to payoff the outstanding balance immediately. I have reluctantly decided to exit the company rather than trying to move the loan. I'm tired of the business and simply want to cash out."

"Who is the investor?" Elmore asked is a firm tone.

Peter realized his best move was to be completely open with Elmore. "An outfit out of Chicago named Venture Funding," Peter shot back without hesitation.

"Shit! Isn't Venture Capital Marler McAdams' company? He's nothing but a scumbag bottom fisher. What sort of bank were you dealing with? No one in their right mind sells a customer down the river to a shady outfit like Venture Funding."

"So you've heard of him," Peter replied sadly.

"Damn straight. Now I understand why you need the money so quickly."

Peter moved in for the kill. "Do we have a deal?"

Elmore didn't immediately respond. He continued to discuss Marler McAdams. "That's the way this bastard operates. He bribes unsuspecting bankers to sell him notes of good companies and then he quickly moves in and forecloses before they can react. The owners are on the street before they know what happened. I'm surprised you don't remember that a couple of years ago there was a big stink about him in the paper over a deal gone bad in Cleveland."

"Fuck!" Peter shouted in the phone. "That's exactly what has happened to me. This scumbag is clever and yes he does move very fast."

"I certainly understand why you need to move quickly. I am confident that we can get to a deal and fund it without a lot of wasted effort, but I don't want to conclude anything over the phone. When can you fly to Dallas so we can meet face-to-face to hash out the final agreement?" Elmore asked in a friendly tone. "The sooner you can get here the better."

This was the silver lining that he and Megan had been searching for these past few days. "I can be in your office by noon today."

After the call, Peter leaned back in his chair. A quiet calm quickly settled over him. This was the first good news that he had received since Monday night. He reached for the phone and called Heather on the intercom. "I need to fly to Dallas immediately to meet with Dallas Metro. Call Southwest Airlines and book me on the ten o'clock flight to Love Field."

From his office Woody heard Peter's instructions to Heather so walked into his office unannounced. "Did Elmore like your offer?" he asked.

"He wants to talk in person, but I think he's going for it. He claims Dallas Metro has the credit availability and can close quickly."

"How did you explain to Phil the need to quickly close a deal?" Woody asked.

Since Peter felt that he competently handled the call with Elmore, he boasted to Woody. "I gave it to him straight up and didn't pull any punches. I told him about McAdams. He claimed to know about his tactics and was fine with our quick deadline for getting a deal closed."

"That's great news. Do you want me to call Megan since you are heading out?" Woody asked. "She can stop running around chasing other options."

"I'll call her from my cell."

Without another word, Peter exited the office. Woody slapped him on the back as he passed him heading for the door. Outside the office Peter climbed into his truck and pulled out of the terminal. Almost immediately he flipped open his cell phone and called Megan. "Elmore looks like a go. I'm heading to Hobby to fly to Dallas for a face-to-face meeting to close the deal."

Megan questioned Peter. "Are you sure this guy is legitimate? This could be another wild goose chase. We are quickly running out of time. If I need you, I don't want you unavailable in Dallas."

"Woody told me that TMS looked at a merger with Dallas Metro about ten years ago. He gave me the number and I called. It must be legitimate because he wanted to wait until next week to move forward."

Peter was flush with excitement and Megan needed to bring him back to terra firma. "Candidly, I'm concerned that it was Woody that showed up with this last minute merger deal. Remember he did nothing with those notices from Union Bank. If it was not for his gross inaction, we might not be in this pickle. I know we are not certain whether Woody is in bed with McAdams, but this rabbit out of the hat merger proposal seems all too convenient."

Megan's concerns caused Peter to pause. "This merger option does seem too well timed; however I think I need to explore it to its logical conclusion. It is a quick trip to Dallas. I can be back by the middle of the afternoon if necessary."

BORROWED MONEY

Megan tried once again to get Peter to forgo the merger option out of fear that it was staged. When she realized that Peter was fully committed to continuing discussions with Elmore, she relented. "I will keep working on my end. Has Woody heard anything from the banks?"

"He promised to call them this morning when they open. Do you really think they can get anything done by close of business tomorrow?" Peter asked.

"If either bank can give us a written commitment tomorrow, I know many judges in town that will grant us a stay which is all that we need to stop the auction. They will not let a business fall to liquidation if fresh financing is fully committed."

As Peter weaved in and out of traffic on Highway 59, he again opened his phone to call Woody. "I want you to call me the minute you hear anything from either of the banks. If they are ready to close on a new loan then I will end merger discussions with Elmore."

***

The old style black telephone rang four times before it was answered by a large man sitting behind the desk. "What do you want? We shouldn't be talking. I don't want any record of calls between the two of us."

"I thought it was important that I call you immediately with new information. Union Bank knows about the sale of the note. They will attempt to buy it back to stop the foreclosure and cut their legal liability. Our plans are on the verge of coming apart at the seams."

"So the bank knows. They will never pay the premium necessary to repurchase the note. They are as powerless as Ferrell. No one can move fast enough at this late date to save TMS from liquidation. Tomorrow night we will be downing expensive cognac at Pappas Brothers Steak House in Houston."

CHAPTER 10

The rush hour traffic was all but dissipated as Peter sped well above the posted speed limit toward Hobby Airport, located about eight miles from downtown Houston on the southeast side of the city. He again opened his cell phone and this time called the main number for Union Bank. He asked the operator for Joe Campbell and waited for Campbell to answer. Campbell's secretary answered the phone on the first ring after the transfer. Before she could complete her greeting, Peter spoke. "This is Peter Ferrell calling. I need to speak to Joe Campbell."

Within seconds, Campbell answered his phone. "What can I do for you Peter?" Campbell asked. His tone was casual, almost too casual for a man on a mission to reacquire the improperly sold loan of a significant customer.

"I'm calling for a status update regarding your efforts to repurchase the TMS loan from Venture Funding," Peter said. "When we spoke yesterday in Chicago, you sounded like it could be consummated quickly."

"We have already spoken to Marler McAdams and he wants millions in premium before he will sell us your loan. Candidly, that is something management at this bank will not consider. So my news is not good."

"That is unacceptable," Peter replied with the pitch in his voice starting to rise. "Union Bank put me in this predicament. Union Bank needs to get me out."

"I appreciate your disappointment, but please make an effort to understand our situation," insisted Campbell. "The bank is in a very tenuous position from a legal perspective."

"Your bank has its tit in a ringer, but it will get much worse if I lose control of my company tomorrow afternoon. This problem was precipitated by your officer's actions," Peter stated challenging the bank's position. "Listen Joe, so far our discussion has centered on Union Bank repurchasing the TMS loan from Venture Funding, but there is another possible solution where this matter is defused without anyone taking a bloodbath. Finance my family's purchase of the assets at the auction tomorrow afternoon. That way you get a new loan and we all walk away from the foreclosure with TMS intact. It is essential that you are by my side if we go into foreclosure tomorrow. Otherwise my situation is hopeless," Peter stressed to the reluctant banker.

"The bank can not, well will not, take any action at this time relative to working with you to resolve the problem created by the unfortunate sale of the TMS promissory loan to Venture Funding," Campbell stated in an almost legal staccato. "I'll send you a letter immediately advising you of the bank's decision. That's all I can tell you."

The conversation took a major turn for the worst and it would not be brought back on track over the phone. Before he could say another word, Campbell moved to end further discussion. "I'm sorry Peter but the bank's decision is final." With those few words, Campbell disconnected the call.

Peter's temper exploded as he screamed loudly within the small confines of the cab of his truck. He reached over and pounded his fist on the dash with such force that the faceplate on the radio shattered. He savagely released all of the pent up frustration of the last three days. His rage was total and complete. Peter steered the massive vehicle to the shoulder in a massive cloud of dust and slammed the shift lever into park. With a flick of his wrist, he killed the engine and removed the key from the ignition switch.

He jumped from the cab and ran around to the opposite side of the truck to the grassy area beyond the shoulder. Standing away from the passing traffic, he screamed out then pounded on the bed of the truck causing the sheet metal to buckle. With his rage in total command of his thoughts, Peter paced back and forth the full length of the truck as he screamed and waved his arms wildly. As he walked on the shoulder, his shoes kicked up a small cloud of dust. The roar of the passing traffic all but muffled the screams of his tantrum. After a few minutes, he started to regain his composure and clear thinking began to return. He decided to go back to the cab before someone stopped to assist him only to discover that he was merely venting his anger. As the cars whizzed by his truck, Peter eased back into the driver's seat. He restarted the vehicle and slowly returned to the freeway.

Once he reached freeway speed, he opened his cell phone and called Megan. "Campbell says McAdams wants millions in premium for our loan. Therefore the bank is unwilling to do anything at this juncture. I think they fear that we are going to sue them, so they want to minimize their losses."

"They have every right to be scared. It is my intention to sue the crap out of them when this is over. I do not understand why they didn't have internal procedures to prevent this sort of thing from happening. Frankly, their decision not to act at this time doesn't surprise me. They are in a deep hole regardless of whether they repurchase our loan or not," Megan said confidently. "I can call Joe if you like and see if we can craft some language to protect them if they would like to work with us to resolve this matter."

Peter shot back, "I'm in my truck on the way to the airport. I will swing by the bank and meet with him."

Megan's legal training immediately kicked into high gear. "As your legal counsel, I am advising you in the strongest terms not to do that. I don't want you to take any action, regardless of how well intentioned, that will prejudice our case when we get these bastards on the defensive in civil court."

"I know what I'm doing," Peter said to reassure Megan. "I just want to see if I can change his mind. Use a little personal charm to win him to my point of view."

"Don't waste precious time with Union Bank. It's a dead end. You don't have any minutes to spare."

"It will only take a few minutes. Besides, I've already taken the off ramp into downtown." Peter maneuvered his truck once again onto the Milam Street garage and parked on the fifth floor. As he exited the elevator on the eighth floor of Union Bank, he saw Joe Campbell pass down one of the halls. Instinctively, Peter called out for

Campbell. Upon hearing his name, Joe turned and although clearly surprised to see Peter, walked briskly to the spot where Peter stood.

"What are you doing here?" Campbell asked looking uneasy with this unscheduled encounter. "The bank cannot help you in this matter. If you need anything further, have Megan call the bank's attorney. Our decision is final so please leave immediately."

"Your position is quite clear. The reason for my visit is to ask if I can pay the premium McAdams is demanding, but to do so I will need the bank to advance me the funds and allow me some time to repay. With the injection of new funds we can all get clear of this quagmire. We can sort through the details next week. If you don't raise your finger to help me out of this situation, I can guarantee that we will all end up in court where blame will be assigned and we will extract our pound of flesh!" Peter stressed his voice now carrying well down the otherwise quiet halls of the bank.

"Come with me," Campbell insisted as he directed Peter to his office. "You were starting to make a scene and I don't want other bank customers to hear you." Once the two men were in his office, Campbell closed the door. "Please leave this building immediately. Don't force me to call security."

It was now obvious to Peter that Campbell was unyielding in his position and unwilling to discuss the matter. Regardless, Peter desperately needed answers to several questions. He pressed Campbell. "Yesterday, you told me you would investigate the matter and all would be fine. Today, I am hearing a very different story. What has changed in a day?"

"Plenty has changed. We did some investigation on Deutsch and independently verified that he got into trouble in Cleveland several years ago for pulling the same stunt."

"Does he have any ideas about how we can deal with McAdams to resolve this matter," Peter asked.

"Jeff Deutsch is no longer employed at Union Bank. He was escorted from the premises first thing this morning. As required by banking laws we contacted the FBI. They intend to conduct a full investigation. We believe that at the end of the day, you will come out financially whole. Therefore it is not critical that we take any actions at this time."

"I may well survive this incident, but my company won't. How do I save my family's business?" Peter demanded.

"Peter, management at the bank is already up to our asses in legal troubles on this one. I'm telling you this because of our longstanding business relationship. If my legal department knew I was talking to you now, I too would be escorted out the door. Deutsch really shoved us into an untenable predicament. I believe he will likely serve time," Campbell disclosed. "For the last time, please leave."

"So you are telling me that my only course of action with the bank is to sue?"

"You and your attorney can do whatever you think is best. Our lawyers are recommending that we fight this out in court if necessary. It is their opinion that we can't fix the problem that Jeff Deutsch created. I've already told you too much."

"Will the bank reconsider its position?"

"I'm sorry Peter, the answer is no!"

CHAPTER II

Peter returned to his truck and looked at his watch. It was nine forty-five. There is no way that he could catch the ten o'clock Southwest flight to Dallas. He called Heather to move his reservation to the ten thirty flight. He also instructed her to contact Phil Elmore to advise him of the slight delay. With any luck, he would have no problem making the later flight. Once on the freeway, he again called Megan. After he told her about his conversation with Campbell, he was surprised to discover that she was calm and unconcerned about Union Bank's unyielding position.

"I don't like the stand they are taking, but I must agree with the legal advice the bank is receiving. They are in a world of hurt. Regardless of what happens tomorrow, I am certain we will see them in court before the end of the year," Megan stated. "Are you still going to Dallas?"

"I've moved my flight to ten thirty. If all goes well, I will be back by late afternoon and we can celebrate the merger tonight over dinner," Peter said enthusiastically.

Megan did not share Peter's optimism. "If you don't mind, I will save my celebrating until the deal is inked and funded."

"Have you verified the errors in the bank's liens?" Peter asked as he swerved through traffic on the Gulf Freeway. "I would like a solid fall back position in the event Elmore doesn't take the bait."

"The errors have been verified. McAdams' liens are incomplete. He can foreclose, but he will not get all of the assets of TMS. Looks like the valuable assets are free of any liens. I am just about finished preparing a petition to the court to ask for a stay of the foreclosure. Leslie will file it later today requesting a hearing no later than late morning tomorrow. I don't want to cut the timing too close to the foreclosure. I want to get in early, get the order signed so it is in my hand when McAdams arrives at the terminal."

"That sounds terrific. I am concerned that the timing of our different options are starting to conflict. I'm talking to Elmore today, but if your stay is granted, then we don't need to sell," Peter concluded.

"Let's play this by ear and keep all options rolling. We only need to make one decision at a time. Go meet with Elmore and we can evaluate what he offers. Remember, we can delay documents if necessary. I realize it's a crappy thing to do, but then this is a game of hardball and no one handed us a cup to wear."

"And you bitched at me about kicking them in the balls."

"There is no question that a good dose of shoe leather to the balls gets results. What about the other banks?"

Peter laughed under his breath. It was now clear to him that he and Megan were more alike than she would ever admit. "I will call Woody when we are finished here."

Megan outlined their remaining options. "With the Union Bank option now dead, it looks like we are down to three options. You can merge with Elmore, move to another bank or get the stay and start with a new list of action items."

"There is also a fourth option that you proposed the other night," Peter offered. "We can sit back and do nothing and watch McAdams foreclose."

"I don't like that option anymore. I'm now mad at every fucking character in this circle jerk. I want my pound of flesh from someone and I am quickly approaching the point that I don't care whose flesh I get."

In the airport, Peter called Woody for an update on the bank applications. He wasn't sure how long he would be out of range of a cell tower and wanted the latest information that was available. "I realize that I am starting to sound redundant, but have you heard from the banks?" Peter asked. "We're getting down to the wire and my options are narrowing. I want to know what pieces I have left to put into play."

"I spoke to both of the banks about forty-five minutes ago. They are both working feverishly on the proposal and are promising an answer by first thing in the morning tomorrow."

Peter shot back with a definite bite in his tone. "Forty-five minutes ago? I told you to call me the minute you heard anything. I never expected you to go slack on me when the chips are down."

Woody exploded with a vengeance. "I'm here trying to keep the company running. I spent every available second of my time taking care of the fueling problem I told you about the other day. It blew up again this morning after you left for the airport. I've been working with Union Bank's wire transfer department to send out pre-payments to I don't know how many suppliers. The fleet is running now and everything is fine. It has been a massive headache. I understand Deutsch isn't around so I had to work with someone new who doesn't know us. He wanted verification on each and every fucking wire."

Peter apologized to Woody for his callousness. "I know you have been working all out these past few days. I couldn't have done it without you. When I met with Joe Campbell…"

Woody temperament changed to positive upon hearing that Peter spoke to Campbell. "What did he say? Is the bank willing to step up to the plate? I hope you have some good news so we can hold off the auction tomorrow."

"Union Bank is concerned that we will sue them over the sale so they have decided to do nothing," Peter reported. "He confirmed that they fired Deutsch early today. They have also called in the FBI to investigate his actions. Joe mentioned about Jeff's involvement in the Cleveland scam and with this second incident, he will likely serve time."

Woody didn't immediately react to the news. He merely mentioned that the officers and staff at the bank made no acknowledgement of Deutsch's departure.

Peter again apologized to Woody. "Listen, I'm sorry about jumping your case over the banks. I really don't have an excuse for my actions. I value your help and assistance."

"Why do you think Deutsch will do time?"

"When you screw around with a federally-insured financial institution, I think they call it a felony. Why do you ask?"

"Curiosity, that's all it is."

Peter closed his cell phone to disconnect the call. Suddenly, the phone rang. Peter flipped it open and saw that it was Megan calling. He answered the phone with a warning, "Make it quick. They are about to close the door to the plane."

"Play your cards close to the vest with Elmore. I am still concerned that this is a delaying tactic to make us burn up more time. I am continuing to push on all fronts. Get into Dallas Metro and quickly flesh out this deal. If it smells, get back here immediately. We will definitely need to regroup."

"I agree completely. When I return to Houston this afternoon, I will call the two other banks personally and verify what Woody is telling us."

"I thought you were going to call first thing this morning. That way we know whether or not Woody is on our team."

"It's been nonstop since I got up this morning. I haven't had the time to make the calls."

"What do you think about Woody now?" Megan asked Peter. "Has your opinion changed?"

"I want to think he's clean, but the jury remains sequestered," Peter confided.

※※※

"I hear Deutsch is out and the FBI is investigating his actions in the sale of the note," the caller reported.

"So why are you telling me?"

"I'm not doing time over the little I'm making on this transaction," the caller stated emphatically.

"Are you asking for a larger cut?"

"I don't like the direction this is taking. I understood at the start that this was a clean deal."

"You're a smart fellow. You should have known better going in. Everything has a risk. That's why you are so well compensated in these deals."

"I want assurances," the caller demanded.

"There are any. So shut up and keep your eyes open. Ferrell is squirrelly and I want to know his every move. In the future, only call me when you have critical information."

CHAPTER 12

The one-hour flight to Dallas was quiet and uneventful. Since it was a midmorning trip, the plane was less than half-filled. Peter sat alone in his row. He spent much of the time preparing for his meeting with Phillip Elmore, the owner of Dallas Metro Trucking. He had no intention of falling flat on his face as he did with Marler McAdams two days earlier. As he looked out the window he could see that it was shaping up to be a beautiful clear picture perfect day. While it was eighty degrees when he departed Houston, Peter knew from experience it would be ten degrees cooler on the ground in Dallas. He prepared by bringing a light jacket. Outside the window, Peter saw the shimmering downtown buildings of central Dallas come into view. He knew he would soon be on the ground.

When the flight attendant opened the door, Peter scrambled from his seat and elbowed his way into the first group of passengers exiting the plane. He moved swiftly down the concourse dodging departing passengers running to catch their flights. The time lost at the car rental counter was minimal and the ride to the car lot was quick. Peter jumped behind the wheel and decided to use Mockingbird Lane as the shortest route to Interstate 35. As usual, the freeway was packed and moved along far below posted speeds.

The trip to Grand Prairie required less than thirty minutes. As he entered the city's industrial park, Dallas Metro Trucking's sign came into view. As he pulled into the parking lot, Peter glanced at his watch. It was twelve twenty.

Peter was appalled at the sight of Dallas Metro's terminal and warehouses. It was the antithesis of TMS. The badly rundown facility consisted mostly of wood framed structures covered with rusted tin. Peter observed with disgust the condition of the operating equipment. The trucks were filthy dirty and the yard was a mud slough.

There was absolutely no asphalt or concrete anywhere to be found. Potholes littered the entire staging yard. The business office was located in an old mobile home at the back of the yard. As Peter drove through the water-filled potholes, muddy water splashed in all directions. A rotten set of wooden stairs lead to a small deck outside the office. The door to the trailer had a small window located at eyelevel. As he anticipated meeting Elmore, only three words coursed through his consciousness, trailer park trash.

Peter parked his rental unit in front of a dirt-covered sign leaning precipitously to the left. Through the caked mud, he was barely able to make out the words indicating visitor parking. He opened the door and without realizing step down into about three inches of mud and water. Before he completely exited the vehicle, the door to the trailer opened and a tall man stepped out into the sunlight. He moved to the railing and leaned forward. "You must be Peter Ferrell," he shouted. "I would recognize you anywhere. You look just like your father."

Peter looked up and gave a half-hearted wave but said nothing. He soon determined that there was no way to avoid the mud. He stood and casually walked toward the gentleman standing on the deck. As he neared the man, he stretched out his hand and greeted Phillip Elmore. "Thank you for seeing me on such short notice. I can see by all of the activity in the yard that you are an extremely busy man."

Elmore stepped forward, grabbed Peter's hand and shook it violently. "The pleasure is mine. I'm flattered that you are giving me the opportunity to acquire TMS. It's a fantastic business that I know many of my competitors would kill for this opportunity to acquire. Come on inside so we can talk."

Inside the trailer, Elmore introduced Peter to one Dallas Metro employee after another. All of the attention made Peter feel like visiting royalty. The staff was cordial and asked Peter many questions about Houston and TMS. Peter repeatedly looked at his watch as the minutes then half hours evaporated. Soon he was concerned whether Elmore would ever take him to his office to discuss business.

It was one thirty when the two men finally moved into Elmore's office. Before Peter could sit, Elmore brought up lunch. "I was thinking we could go to my favorite lunch club in downtown Dallas for bite to eat."

The endless stream of introductions took their toll on Peter's amiable disposition. It was time to talk business and Peter wanted no further delays. Lunch was not high on his list of priorities so he responded coldly to Elmore's invitation. "That is a wonderful offer, but I would like to move into our discussion regarding the merger. As I indicated on the phone, time is critical. We have already lost a significant amount of time."

Elmore ignored Peter's insistence that the conversation progress into the purpose for the trip. With exuberance he continued on his insistence that the two men share a meal. "I can have my receptionist order us some sandwiches from the gourmet deli down the road. While we are waiting for them to be delivered, I would like give you a tour of my operation."

Further resistance now appeared futile. Peter didn't want to appear unappreciative to his white knight, so he reluctantly agreed to the tour. Peter and Phil gave their lunch requests to the office receptionist who looked to be no older than sixteen. They walked to the terminal, sloshing through the mud to the main warehouse building. Inside, men were shouting and trash littered every square inch of floor space. Spills were common and broken pallets were scattered indiscriminately. The anarchy didn't seem to faze Elmore or his crew. He walked around nonstop pointing out numerous features which did not interest Peter in the least.

After about an hour, Peter and Elmore returned to the trailer. As they entered, Elmore grabbed a large white bag from the corner of the receptionist's desk. They once again entered Elmore's office and over a cluttered card table, consumed sandwiches, chips and sodas. When they finished, Elmore gathered the trash, stuffed it into the bag then tossed it into a large trashcan in the corner of the office. "Two points," he shouted as the bag fell into the trash. It was at that time that Peter realized that the food came from a local convenience store, so much for the receptionist going to a gourmet deli down the road to buy lunch. Once again the words trailer park trash passed through Peter's mind.

Peter looked at his watch. It is already three thirty. Time was quickly passing so he decided to press Elmore to open conversation about their impending transaction. "We need to talk about the elements of the sale of TMS to Dallas Metro."

Elmore moved to the leather executive chair behind his desk. He cleared his throat and looked directly at Peter. "With those contracts of yours, I will become major force in this region and with the addition of your terminal in Houston. I will soon be in other key markets all the way to Miami."

"I knew it was a good fit. And you have to agree the price is fair," Peter emphasized. "I trust the money can be funded as early as tomorrow."

"Money is no problem. I confirmed availability with my bank before you arrived. So what is your final price," Elmore asked as he flashed a sinister look.

Peter immediately noticed a slight change in Elmore's demeanor, as he seemed to retreat into a defensive posture. He was confused why Elmore would once again ask about price. Peter was certain they mutually agreed upon the number before he accepted the trip to Dallas. "The price remains at thirty million dollars. I thought we had agreement on the number earlier and that my trip today was merely a formality to answer any questions you have about TMS."

"I thought you might be willing to come off your number a tad. There is no question that your company is worth every penny, but I seem to be in the driver's seat. You need money quickly and my check will clear. I think you owe me a break especially since I've been through this dog and pony routine with you guys once before," Elmore said in a gruff voice.

"I don't know what kind of game you are playing, but I came here in good faith to close on a sale. If you are not interested in my company, then I guess these discussions are ended and I will immediately return to Houston."

"Don't get your panties in a wad. I'm fully committed to acquiring your company. I just don't want to pay your price," Elmore said with an evil smile starting to form across his face.

"That's the price, thirty million. And trust me I'm not negotiating on the price. It's the jewel that will catapult you into a leadership role in this region."

Elmore suddenly changed the subject. "How was your lunch?" he asked with a grin.

By this point, Peter had grown tired of Elmore's games. He responded tersely, "Best convenience store sandwich I ever ate. Actually, I can't say that I ever enjoyed a sandwich from a convenience store before today."

"I'm glad the sandwich was to your liking. Consider it your last meal at TMS. I'm going buy your company alright, but for a sum a great deal less than thirty million."

"Sorry, but less isn't going to do it."

"I never said that my plan was to buy TMS from you," Elmore stated confidently as he released a loud menacing laugh. "I plan to buy your company at auction tomorrow afternoon. Once the auctioneer starts the bidding, the price will be far less than the thirty million dollars you are asking."

Peter remained silent for a few seconds as he digested Elmore's statements. "I don't understand," Peter stumbled. "I thought we had a deal."

"What's so difficult to figure out? Let me make it easy for your pea brain. I'll be at the auction tomorrow with my check book in hand to buy your company for a song."

"So you are working with McAdams," Peter shouted as he stood from his chair and moved near Elmore. "If you wanted to screw me, why couldn't you do it over the phone?"

"I wanted the pleasure of seeing the reaction on your face when you figured out that you have been screwed like a cheap whore." Elmore let out a loud roar. "And as far as working with that slim bucket McAdams, he's out to screw both of us. He only thinks that I'm on his side," he revealed. "But then he's an idiot. I'm more of an independent contractor in this transaction."

"So there is truly no honor among crooks," Peter nearly screamed.

"Never has been," Elmore chuckled.

"How did you ever get involved in this deal?"

"That putz McAdams called up six months ago and said he could deliver your company on a silver platter for a premium price. He must really think I'm stupid. His plan is to close this deal out quickly with a prepackaged sale at the auction. However, the man is an idiot and hasn't worked to develop a competitive market. I'm the only buyer he has lined up. At the sale, I don't have to come to the table with all my money. He will soon find out that Chicago is not the center of the universe. Come down to Texas, you better be ready for a good old-fashioned knife fight. I have no plans to pay what the company is worth."

Peter was furious but unfortunately he was cornered. His only move was to immediately leave Dallas Metro and return to Houston. His mind could not assemble any meaningful response to Elmore. Out of sheer desperation he blurted, "Fuck you!"

"How original!" Elmore roared with laughter. "Now you get the fuck out of my office!"

CHAPTER 13

Outside Dallas Metro's offices, Peter returned to his rental car and kicked the mud from his shoes. He jumped inside, slammed the door with a loud thud, shoved the key hard into the ignition and sped quickly out of the parking lot. He looked down at his watch and realized that it was already four thirty. As he looked in the rearview mirror, he saw Phil Elmore standing outside the trailer happily waving goodbye. Once again valuable time was lost forever.

Peter removed his cell phone from his belt and called Heather. He instructed her to move his return flight to five thirty. The traffic would be building in preparation of rush hour, so he calculated it would take about forty-five minutes to drive back to Love Field and return the rental car.

As he drove toward the airport, Peter could only see red. His mind was churning at full throttle with waves of anger coursing through ever fiber of his body. Never before had he been filled with so much pure rage. This delay was the most damaging of all. Another full day lost, time that he could have used to aggressively attack other options. This trip was another well-planted misstep in a well-orchestrated plot to gain control of TMS.

It was now clear that since Monday night, both he and Megan had run around in circles chasing their own tails. If they couldn't immediately take the offense and gain momentum, the game was all but over. No question about it, there was a puppet master somewhere controlling all of the strings. If he didn't get his ass in gear, this shadowy figure may not come out into the light of day until after the auction at which time it will be too late.

Before boarding the plane, Peter called Megan. He brought her up to date on the meeting with Elmore. She refrained from reminding Peter that she was against to trip from the beginning. Like Peter she too realized that her mouth more often than not was her single greatest liability in their relationship. She then disclosed to Peter that she had completed her final review of all of Union Bank's security filings with the county clerk's office. Her initial findings have been confirmed. The petition she drafted requesting a stay from the auction was filed with the court around noon and she expected to have a hearing no later than early afternoon on Friday. Leslie was on her way to the county clerk's office to see if a time had been posted for the hearing.

"Have you spoken to your mother and uncle?" she asked. "It is critical that we have their full support if we have any prayer of succeeding. Once McAdams starts the foreclosure auction, it's all over."

"I plan to drive directly from the airport to see each of them upon my return to Houston. I don't think I will have any problem getting them to signup, especially since we now know that Elmore is integral to McAdams' overall plan."

"You sound tired," Megan said softly. "Have you had any rest since Monday? I don't need you dropping dead in your tracks."

"You were right; the trip to Dallas was a bust. I wasted another day chasing a rabbit down an endless hole. We are near the end of the game and our bag of tricks is nearly empty."

"We are not out of the game yet. There is still the possibility of the stay as well as the other banks. Have you heard anything from Woody?" Megan inquired. "I am finally starting to believe he is working for the enemy. He has failed us repeatedly since Monday night."

"He didn't leave me a message on my phone. I don't know where his head is. This is damn important and he doesn't seem to be pressing the banks for a decision."

"I can call them right now," Megan offered. "You are trying to get on the plane."

"Let me call Heather right now and get the phone numbers. I will call the banks myself when I hit the ground in Houston."

After Peter disconnected the phone, he called Bill Cobb, TMS' corporate controller. Bill answered his phone on the first ring. "Bill, this is Peter calling. I have some questions about our compliance with Union Bank's loan covenants. Can you help me?" Peter asked.

"As you might remember I track our performance each month to the various loan covenants. With a few minor exceptions, we are in compliance."

Peter's voice exploded with excitement. "Do I understand you correctly that we have no violations?"

With the blandness of an accountant, Bill clarified his statement to Peter. "There are several violations in minor areas."

"Have you spoken to Union Bank about the violations?" Peter inquired.

"When the letters started about six months ago, I called Deutsch and he told me to ignore them. He claimed they were documenting their files. Since the violations were not of a financial nature, then the bank had no plans to call the loan."

"That is great news. Did you ever get that in writing?"

"I asked him for written confirmation. Unfortunately he never got around to sending it to me."

***

As the gate attendant called for final boarding, Peter called Heather's direct line. To his dismay all he got was her voice mail. He decided to leave her a message to pull up the numbers and have them ready upon his return to Houston. He was emphatic that she was not to mention anything about his requests to Woody. Once on the plane he mapped out his schedule for the precious few hours remaining before the auction. There were a thousand things to complete and not nearly enough minutes in which to complete more than a few.

The moment the Southwest flight touched down in Houston, Peter turned on his phone and immediately called Heather. "Do you have the numbers I need," Peter asked.

"I never heard of these guys," she insisted. "Are you sure Woody sent them packages on Tuesday?" Heather asked. "I never sent anything out as you described."

"What!" Peter screamed. "He told me that he gave you several packages to send to the banks in town."

"I didn't send anything out this week for Woody," Heather said confidently. "I think I would remember sending out three or four thick packages."

"Trust me Woody sent several packages out on Tuesday. I want you to pull the courier receipts."

"Woody didn't send anything," Heather insisted. "I would know if he had because I have my register in front of me. The last package sent out was last week and I have the next receipt number in my file to be issued. Nothing has gone out. Let me check with Woody."

"No," Peter yelled into the phone. "Don't talk to Woody!"

"Do you still want the phone numbers for the banks?" she asked. "I pulled them from the phone book."

"Damn straight!"

Peter disconnected the call with Heather then called the number for John Bailey at Houston National Bank. Bailey answered his phone on the first ring. Peter did not waste time with needless pleasantries. "This is Peter Ferrell with Transportation Management Services. Woody Coppell spoke to you recently about moving our loan to your institution. I'm calling to see when you expect to be ready with an answer and can issue a formal commitment letter. Woody would normally be checking with you, but he has been working on several special projects for me."

"Houston National Bank would love to talk to you about becoming one of our customers. Can you put together some information on TMS then call me so I can schedule a time that is convenient for both of us to meet and discuss your company's needs?" Bailey insisted sounding pleased with the call.

"I think you have misunderstood what I said. I believe Woody spoke to you earlier in the week and delivered a package of information on Tuesday. It is my understanding that your bank has been analyzing my company's financial information for several days now," Peter shot back becoming perturbed with Bailey's slowness.

"I haven't seen or spoken to Woody since I saw him at a Chamber of Commerce luncheon about three months ago. At that time I asked if we could take a look at your business. He waved me off and I haven't heard from him since, least of all earlier this week."

Peter immediately hung up the phone ending his conversation with Bailey. He then called Dave Fields at Texas Merchants Bank. His story was virtually identical to that of Bailey. He too had not heard from Woody in months. Peter immediately called Megan. He screamed into the phone when she answered, "He's dirty! The fucking bastard is dirty."

"Who on earth are you talking about?" she asked.

"It's confirmed. Woody is working against us," Peter revealed. "Both banks told me that he never sent them anything. In fact, they haven't spoken to Woody for months. He has been sitting in front of us and feeding us one lie after another!"

Megan pondered on the news for almost a minute. "It's good that we now know this," Megan offered. "Thank god we never told him any of the details of our findings and our petition to the court."

Megan could sense Peter's anger through the telephone. His breathing was heavy and deep. "All dead ends, we have run full speed down too many dead ends. Under Woody's deliberate direction, we have been spinning our wheels. All part of a master plan, but whose master plan?"

CHAPTER 14

It took Peter nearly an hour to drive the short distance from Hobby Airport to the corner of San Felipe Road and Kirby Drive in the heart of the exclusive River Oaks section of Houston. About one hundred feet from the busy light at the intersection he pulled onto a tile covered drive leading to an exclusive thirty-six story private condominium development. He eased his large truck near the window of a stone covered guard station. A well-dressed security officer opened the sliding window in the station and looked up at Peter. Without hesitation, Peter spoke to the guard. "Peter Ferrell to see my Uncle Stuart Ferrell," Peter stated emphatically. "His unit is on the twenty-ninth floor."

"Is he expecting you?" the guard asked showing no emotion on his face.

"No, he doesn't know I'm coming by," Peter responded. "I do have a key and I am authorized to enter the residence."

"I will call Mr. Ferrell and tell him you are coming up." Without another word, the guard pushed on a small white button under the desk which caused the massive wrought iron gate to open in one broad sweep. "Park to the right," he directed then closed the window.

Peter did as instructed, locked his truck and entered the elevator lobby. When he arrived on the twenty-ninth floor, he turned to the right and walked past five ornate doors. He looked at the brass plate affixed to the sixth door. Compared to the entry doors to the other units on the floor, this door was extremely plain. The words printed on the polished plate were simple and plain.

Stuart Ferrell
2903

Peter was uncertain exactly how his uncle would react to the news about the loan sale and he and Megan's efforts these past few days to save the company. Stuart was John Ferrell's older brother and together with Peter represented the only living blood relatives remaining in the family. At one time he was active in the trucking company but exited the business shortly before the sudden death of his brother. Several attempts had been made through the years to get him to return to an active role in the business, but they were all unsuccessful. His reasons for not returning to TMS had never been fully disclosed to Peter. Stuart lived comfortably having saved his money over the years. In addition, his ten percent interest in TMS paid him a handsome annual dividend.

Peter gathered his courage and raised his fist stopping just short of the door. Before he struck a single blow, the door suddenly opened with a whoosh. Stuart Ferrell stepped from behind the door and addressed his nephew, "I didn't expect to see you of all people today. You never call or come by to see me. I hope you are not calling asking for money," Stuart said with a laugh. He reached out, grabbed Peter by the arm and pulled him into the condominium. "Can I get you a drink?"

"I could use a cold one. It's been a long week."

"That's why I exited the business years ago. Every week was a long week. After a while the weekdays became blurred with the weekends and I never knew if I was coming from or going to that damn terminal. In the trucking business you constantly live behind the eight-ball and all of your customers are constantly plotting to screw you however they can. I don't know how you have stayed in it. To be truthful, I originally thought you were too soft for the goons, but it looks like I was wrong. What has it been, ten years now?"

Stuart invited Peter to sit in the living room while he retrieved a couple of cold beers from the refrigerator. While Stuart was out of the room, Peter moved to the full-length windows on the far side of the room. He pulled back the curtains and looked outside. In the near distance rose the downtown skyline of Houston. This west side view of the city was by far the best. As Stuart walked back into the room, Peter started to talk to his uncle. "You have the finest view of the city. If this was my condominium, I would keep these curtains open all day long."

"This time of the year the morning heat is unbearable. I generally open the curtains about noon and close them when I retire in the evening. I was too lazy to open them today. As to the view, it is available to anyone, but I have to warn you, the price is rather steep. As you know I was one of the first tenants in this complex fifteen years ago. These babies are selling for four to five times what I paid back then."

"It is worth every penny, then and now."

After a few more pleasantries and swigs from the beers, Peter updated his uncle on the unfortunate events of the week.

"I never did liked those bastards at Union Bank and tell me, why on earth would you ever go and visit Phil Elmore. The guy is a crook of the highest order," Stuart revealed. "I wouldn't let Dallas Metro haul my garbage."

"Woody told me to go and see the guy," Peter disclosed. "According to him it would be a match made in heaven."

"Woody knows the guy is a crook. He tried to make an end around move on John about ten years ago. When your father found out, he cut some deals that nearly bankrupted Dallas Metro. He has no love for TMS or the Ferrell family."

"Woody told me that Dad declined a merger offer because he wanted me to eventually run the company."

"That's a crock of shit. Elmore came in and threatened to move into our territory unless John sold out for a song. It had absolutely nothing to do with you. What's wrong with Woody?" Stuart asked. "He knows all of the facts surrounding that period of time. Has he been hitting the bottle again?"

"I believe Woody is dirty and not only that but also that he is working with someone to complete the liquidation of TMS."

"Well, I never liked the guy personally. I always found him to be just too creepy. I think there is a lot more in his closet that a large collection of skeletons."

"But why would he sell us out?" Peter asked his uncle. "We have treated him very well for many years."

"Maybe he needed money," Stuart speculated. "A number of years ago, he got in trouble with the ponies and we had to bail him out. At that time I thought he learned his lesson and would never return to the window. But addictions really fuck up your mind."

"I never knew he had a gambling problem. What else have I not been told?"

"You're not here to talk about Woody. What's going to happen to the company?"

"I think Megan and I will be able to save the company. She has several irons in the fire and we aren't going to let a few unsavory bastards take us down."

"Why fight it son? Let the damn thing go. It isn't worth. You should have enough money saved by now to start a new business."

Peter let out a heavy sigh. "I know you never liked the company, but I have an obligation to ensure its survival."

Stuart shook his from side to side with visible disgust. "Why in heaven's name do you think you are under some kind of moral obligation to save TMS? Where did you ever get an idea like that?'

"Grandpa started it and Dad worked himself to death to keep it alive. You and mom never understood that. This company defines the Ferrell family in this state. And I'm not going to let it go without a fight."

Stuart stood and moved near Peter on the large sofa. He rested his hand softly on Peter's knee. "There is a great deal of factual information you are missing about your family and TMS. Your grandfather was a fun loving guy. He started the business on a lark frankly because the trucking business was all he knew. He started out as a truck driver and grew from there. Dewey thoroughly enjoyed the business because he was able to be around all of his friends and cronies. He never considered it work. The business rarely made money and actually floundered under his leadership. It had several near misses with bankruptcy before your father joined."

Stuart could see the clear look of surprise on Peter's face. The news shook him to his very core. "So why did my dad dedicate every waking moment to the business."

"Because that's the way he was. I never knew anyone else so driven."

"He knew that my mom hated the business. Yet he continued. Why?" Peter asked. "Why didn't he simply walk away and save his marriage? Sell out and go fishing."

Stuart laughed loudly, "I can't see John Ferrell fishing. He didn't have the patience to wait for fish to bite." He reached over and held Peter's arm. "Your mom hated your dad, not TMS. Your dad was as stubborn as they come. The business was his life. He had something to prove in his life."

"To Grandpa?"

"No Peter, to himself. Valerie never understood the unbelievable drive that was John's nature. He was blessed with extraordinary ambition but it was as much a curse. His drive had nothing whatsoever to do with the trucking business. He would have been that way if he had sold hotdogs from a vending cart downtown at the corner of Milam and Lamar. At the end of the day Valerie married the wrong man."

Peter was shocked by the torrent of revelations unleashed by his uncle. The information totally contradicted everything he had believed since he was a teenager. In an instant his love for his father shifted from deep love to searing hatred.

"You have nothing to prove to anyone, much less to a couple of dead guys. This is your life for you to live. Don't try to relive theirs."

"But I need to save TMS from the auctioneer's gavel."

"I told you, let it go," Stuart insisted. "It's just a hard dirty highly competitive business. Good riddance. I can assure you that I for one don't miss the awful smell of diesel."

"After everything that you have told me tonight, I think I'm just about ready to make that decision. Still you have to understand, there is a great deal of excess value in the company. I'm not going to abandon that value and let some piker scoop it up with virtually no effort. The precious blood and sweat of our family is worth too much."

"Have you thought about a white knight?" Stuart asked sounding more upbeat. "Do you have time?"

"That's why I went to see Elmore."

Stuart thought for a few minutes then issued instructions to Peter. "Let's call Martin Ivey. He's a good guy if there ever was one. He owns Coastal Truckers in Galveston. I still keep in contact with him and he has said on more than one occasion that he would love to put the two companies together. I know I have his number around here somewhere."

After rummaging through a large desk in an adjoining study, Stuart returned with a single business card." He immediately called the number on the card and spoke to the receptionist at Coastal. She informed him that Martin Ivey was out of town attending a funeral but would return to the office in the morning. She agreed to leave a note advising Ivey that Peter would be calling to discuss a possible sale of TMS.

Peter thanked his uncle for his help and support. "I'm glad I stopped by this evening. You have cleared up a lot of long standing misconceptions about many things that I have dragged around with me for too many years."

"What else can I do for you?"

"One of our options is to attempt to buy the company at the foreclosure auction but we don't have sufficient financial backing. Megan and I could use some help."

"I'm out of TMS for good and will not put up another dime even if it is to save the company. Ask me for anything else."

"If the company goes down in total as we fear is possible, you will lose the dividends off your company stock. Can you live comfortably without them?"

"I will make by just fine."

"I may need you to sign a proxy for your ten percent of the company. We may have to make some eleventh hour maneuvers tomorrow if we have any hope of walking away with cash after the auction."

"I will sign whatever you need," Stuart assured his nephew.

"There appears to be too many outsiders taking a run at acquiring TMS. I thought my battle was only with Marler McAdams. Now, I'm not sure exactly how big or organized the opposition is. This is our company and if we decide to let it go, we are walking away with our pockets chocked full of compensation. If I throw in the towel and punch-out of TMS for good, I'm grabbing every penny I can get my hands on. Megan is drafting the proxy as we speak."

"What time is the auction?" Stuart asked.

"Five o'clock."

"I will be here all day tomorrow. She can come by at whatever time is convenient."

"What does Valerie say about all of this? I know she's going to be a tough sell on anything."

"She's my next stop."

Stuart grimaced. "I wouldn't want to be in your shoes."

CHAPTER 15

Peter returned to his truck and prepared to leave to visit his mother and bring her up to speed on the developments of the week. By Houston standards it was a short four-mile drive to the Westside neighborhood of Tanglewood where Valerie Ferrell lived. He sat quietly in the cab of his truck for several minutes digesting Stuart's astonishing revelations. Peter felt as if his world was somehow thrown into a high-speed blender in the brief time since he arrived at his uncle's condominium. His comfortable understanding of so many long-held facts was suddenly torn apart and indiscriminately thrown into a heap of Ferrell family discontent. He had no warning and was therefore completely unprepared for Stuart's disclosures.

Anxiety over visiting his mother overtook Peter him with vengeance. Would he learn more secret Ferrell family truths, truths he was unsure whether he wanted to know? The last four days presented Peter with an almost insurmountable challenge to save his company. Thanks to Stuart, all of the interfamily relationships under which Peter lived his whole life were now shuffled beyond any recognition. The touchstones by which he steadied life all these years were sudden nowhere to be found.

After Peter started his truck, the clock in the middle of the dash illuminated, displaying eight o'clock. McAdams' auction would bring the curtain down on TMS in a little over twenty-one hours. Peter placed his truck into reverse and backed out of the visitor parking. Once again drove his truck up to the large gate at the entrance of the complex.

To his surprise, it did not open automatically in response to his truck. At first he thought that he had missed the electronic trigger buried in the drive. Then he saw the security guard peek through the window to the guardhouse and within seconds the massive gate started to move. "Great security," Peter whispered under his breath. As he passed the guardhouse, he observed the guard watching him exit. His face was expressionless.

From his uncle's complex, Peter drove west on San Felipe Road. By this time of the evening, rush hour traffic long ago subsided. About three quarters of a mile outside the West Loop, he turned right on Yorktown Drive and almost immediately made a hard left onto Fieldwood Drive. At the third house on the right, Peter drove onto a large curved drive directly in front of a sixty-year-old ranch style house. The house was built in the forties and was one of the few remaining original structures in the area. It was clearly evident from the overall condition of the house that it had never been updated. The value of the property was slowly declining to the underlying value of the real estate. Peter shook his head from side to side in recognition that he would have to liquidate the property in a few years when his mother moved into an assisted living facility. There was no question that the buyer would immediately demolish the structure so that a new modern home could be erected in its place.

Peter stepped down from his truck and stood motionless in the front yard for several minutes. He listened to the sounds on the street and recalled the years when he played throughout the neighbor as a child. It was a different neighborhood when Peter lived here. All of the houses of his friends had long been replaced with large imposing structures with high fences and elaborate security systems. On many evenings he waited at this very spot for his father to return from the TMS terminal so they could share the games of normal fathers and sons. All too often, his father did not return before it was time for Peter to go inside and complete his homework.

As he stood and passed his shoes through the tall grass, Peter realized that he possessed few childhood memories of happy times. There was always a great deal of sadness in this old structure and every fiber of Peter's being screamed for him to jump back into the truck and speed away. After one last glance across the neighborhood, Peter walked around the back of his truck and approached the front door to the house.

Valerie Farrell refused to maintain a normal and ongoing relationship with her son. She blamed the trucking company for killing her husband, a man she loved too completely at one time. Through the last will and testament of her husband, she received considerable money, the house in Tanglewood and 41% of the stock in Transportation Management Services. Peter received only the 49% of the ownership stock in TMS and nothing else. The division of the stock was designed to prevent Peter from having complete control of the company while his mother was alive. John Ferrell wanted to ensure that the company remained viable so it could provide both his wife and his brother with steady cash flow to meet their needs for the remainder of their lives. All decisions required the cooperation of two of the three owners, Valerie, Stuart and Peter.

Valerie Ferrell's hatred for TMS was complete. She believed it was responsible for the premature death of her husband and eventually would take her son from her. Within hours of John Ferrell's death, she begged Peter to sellout. If Peter didn't want to sell, then she pleaded for them to shutter the business and liquidate the property and equipment. Within the first year following John Ferrell's death, the demands of TMS upon his time created a permanent riff between Peter and his mother.

Peter stepped up to the front door and rang the doorbell. He had no key to the house. It was years since he visited his mother on a social basis. They spoke on the phone even more infrequently. The only times that Peter came to the house was to deliver documents for his mother to sign. Most of the owners' meetings for TMS were held over the phone. Peter's mother had not been to the terminal since before the death of her husband.

Peter rang the doorbell a second time. Suddenly he heard movement within the house. Shortly the housekeeper opened the door and smiled upon seeing Peter. She stepped forward and gave him a huge bear hug. "It is so good to see you Peter," she cried. "I can't remember the last time you were here. You should have let me know you were coming. I could have fixed supper for you."

"Is my mother here?" Peter asked with a heavy sigh. "I have some important business to discuss with her."

"She is in her room watching the television," the housekeeper replied. "Go into the kitchen and I will let her know you are here."

Peter walked into the kitchen as he observed the housekeeper walking down the hall toward his mother's room. He opened the refrigerator and peeked inside. He saw nothing of interest. Without a man in the house, there was no need for Valerie to stock beer and soft drinks. Peter walked to the pantry and peered inside, more of the same nothingness.

Within a few minutes, Peter's mother entered the kitchen wearing her nightclothes. She did not come near him nor did she offer a kiss or a hug. Her total coldness was overwhelming. She selected a chair at the table then sat quietly never uttering a welcoming word. For a few minutes Peter stood in complete silence at the tile-covered island in the middle of the room. He sighed deeply then reluctantly moved to the table taking the chair directly across from his mother.

"Obviously, you came here to tell me something," she started tersely. "You already know I have no interest in what you are going to tell me. I know it has something to do with the terminal and I don't care."

"You never make this easy for me do you?" Peter said with a clear tinge of anger in his tone. "Will you ever let this die?"

Valerie turned her head to the side to stare at the floor and refused to say anything further. The little voice in Peter's head told him to stand and walk away forever. Walk out of his mother's life permanently. Valerie was an angry old woman hardened and unyielding in her position. Her hatred for the business was unconditional and no amount of effort by her son would make even the slightest dent in her position.

"You are correct Mother. I came here to tell you about some recent developments affecting the future of the terminal and as a result the future of the family's financial condition. Union Bank sold our loan to a Chicago-based investment company who is planning to take over the company tomorrow. If theses bloodsuckers are successful, then what you have wished for all the years since Dad's death will happen. The Ferrell family will no longer own Transportation Management Services."

Valerie looked up and Peter saw tears in her eyes. Her reaction to the news surprised him. He fully expected to see a broad smile across her face. This is the first hint of emotion Peter had seen from her since he was a teenager. "You're right. If we lose the company, I will be happy. I can't wait until you are out on the street. That miserable company ruined my life."

Peter struck back. "The goddamn company didn't ruin your life. You did that all by yourself without help from anyone."

"You don't know what you are talking about," she nearly screamed. "That company took your father away from me."

"Before I came here, I had a long conversation with Stuart. He told me many things that I never understood or appreciated before tonight. I used to believe that this company defined our family and that it should never be changed. Our family is known in this town by our ownership of TMS."

"This town doesn't give a damn about us or TMS. It is all in your mind. Just like your father. You know how much I hate the company!"

"I now understand that no one gives a damn about us or TMS. Regrettably, what I never understood before tonight was that John Ferrell was a driven man and at the end of the day, he would have been the bastard he was whether he ran TMS or some other company."

"Don't you think I know that!" she screamed as she pounded her fists on the table.

Peter sat back in his chair. For several seconds, he could not speak. His mother's acknowledgement of his father's obsession was unexpected. "If you have known all of these years, then why do you hate TMS?" Peter asked. "Why have you made my life a living hell?"

"So you wouldn't be like your father. I thought that if I could get you out of the business, you might be different. But you are just like your father."

"I'm nothing like my father," Peter argued as he stood and walked around the kitchen. "Over these many years I thought it was necessary for me to carry on the family business. However, my dilemma has been that my heart has never been in it. I was only doing it because I thought it was expected. I thought Dad wanted me to carry on for you and Stuart. I accept now that he didn't give a damn about us, and more importantly he didn't care about what I did in my life. With John Ferrell, it was only about John Ferrell."

"So what do you plan to do?" Valerie asked accepting that she may have been wrong about Peter.

"That's why I'm here tonight. I think we are going to lose the company tomorrow and I'm fine with that. I just need your help to make sure that the family walks away with all of the money that we are due. We need to be compensated for what this company has done to our family all these years. I'm ready to leave. I now want to leave but at the same time it is crucial for us to ensure that our contributions and hard work do not simply get flushed down the fucking drain. I don't think you want that either."

Over the succeeding couple of hours, Peter and Valerie discussed the plan that Megan intended to execute to grab the cash in the company. Valerie agreed to let Peter vote her interests if necessary to close the deal. Peter told his mother that he wanted to rekindle their relationship. "It's been too long at time since we have acted like a real family. I think Megan and I will soon be moving to the next level. I want our children to have a grandmother for Christ's sakes."

"Grandchildren," Valerie said as she pushed a wide smile across her face. "I would like that very much."

"Megan has prepared a document that you will need to sign so we can quickly transact our business tomorrow before the auction starts. Either Megan or I will get it to you for your signature."

"I will be here all day."

"I don't know how to thank you," Peter said.

"If this gets us all back together, that is thanks enough. You said you went to see Stuart. How is he doing? I haven't seen him in years."

"We had a great conversation. He really opened my eyes. There were many things I didn't know about Dewey and John."

"This weekend, you and Megan should come over and I can tell many more stories that you have never heard."

"I would like that."

***

"Stuart and Valerie are on board. They will sign whatever you need."

Megan was pleased with the news. "How did it go with your mother?"

"It didn't start out well, but after we opened up, we quickly got on the same page. The period is separation is over."

"That's wonderful news." Megan responded. "Have you eaten?"

"All I've had today is a one crappy convenience store sandwich."

"I can pick up something and meet you at your house."

CHAPTER 16

Megan pulled into the driveway at Peter's house at nine forty-five. She noticed that his truck was parked in front of the house rather than in the garage. She grabbed the bag with the take-out and walked into the house.

"Honey, I'm home," she called as she walked into the kitchen and immediately started to prepare supper.

Within a few minutes Peter entered the kitchen barefooted, wearing blue jeans and a red t-shirt. He grabbed Megan from behind and lifted her slightly. She screeched but did not resist Peter's antics. He spun her around several times as she held tightly to his arms. He then spun her faster causing her to scream in excitement. After she was sufficiently scared, he slowed the spinning and set her down. She turned to face him then reached out and pulled him tightly to her chest. She planted a deep wet kiss on his lips and once again squeezed him tightly. He reached down and squeezed her bottom through her clothes. She moaned in response to his attention.

Peter looked over his shoulder at the food that sat on the counter. "Chinese!" he shouted. "I'm starved."

"I thought you might be hungry for something else," she cooed with a sinister grin. "It has been a while for both of us. I certainly need some romance and I know it wouldn't hurt you at bit."

Without another word, Peter lifted Megan and carried her to the bedroom. They stood for several minutes adjacent to the bed in a passionate embrace. Slowly and ever so delicately, Peter removed Megan's expensive business suit piece by piece. After her skirt fell to the floor, he reached down to remove her thong. To his surprise and absolute delight, he discovered that she was not wearing a thong or anything else under her skirt. She spread her legs slightly in response to his anxious probing fingers and whispered in his ear, "I came prepared."

In one smooth continuous motion, Peter lifted Megan and gently laid her down on the top of the bed with her legs hanging off the edge. Instinctively, she raised her legs, brought her feet onto the surface of the bed then separated her knees wide. Peter caressed Megan's inner thighs then knelt of the floor and gently slid his hands up the sides of Megan's body. She breathed heavily in response to his delicate touch. Upon reaching the full extension of his arms, he brought his hands to her chest and softly cupped each breast. His index fingers carefully crossed the tops of her breasts as he felt the hardness of her nipples. He then lowered his head between her legs, causing her to gasp.

Megan struggled for breath as Peter softly kissed the undersides then insides of her thighs. She moved her right hand from her side and placed it between her legs. Using her long slender fingers in a scissor like she delicately probed her quivering wetness until she found the solitary object of her search. She massaged it gently until it was fully erect. Without removing her right hand from its task, she lifted her left arm and placed her left hand on the back of Peter's head. She tightly grasped a lock of his hair then forcible pulled him forward. When he was positioned where she wanted, she withdrew her right hand and firmly pressed Peter's head deep between her legs. "Make me scream," she purred. "I have been waiting for this for almost a week. I can't wait any longer."

After their passions were quenched, Peter looked over at the clock. It was nearly midnight. He tapped delicately on Megan's shoulder and said, "I think we need to discuss our tactics for tomorrow."

Megan moaned and sat up in the bed. "That was wonderful," she cooed with contentment in her voice. "By now the Chinese food must be cold."

Peter laughed, "That's why I have a microwave. Why don't you take a shower and I will get the food ready."

In the kitchen, Peter heard the water running. He quickly performed the necessary tasks and when all was complete and served,

Megan entered the kitchen. She was wearing a short see through robe with a white thong underneath. "If you don't put on some clothes, we are going to end up right back in the bedroom and never get any work done."

"I know you're enjoying the show, so stop protesting and just keep it in your pants for now. Your friend can come out to play when we are finished."

As the couple sat at the table to eat, they discussed Megan's plan. As always her legal preparation was thorough and she went through her findings in a strictly professional manner. "You were going to determine whether TMS was out of compliance under the loan covenants."

"This afternoon I called Bill Cobb. He says that the violations are minor and that Deutsch told him to ignore the letters. Unfortunately Deutsch would never put it in writing. So we have nothing."

"Another dead end," she started. "Here is where we stand right now. I will go into court tomorrow at two and get this whole cluster fuck stopped dead in its tracks. Then we can work to sell the business in an orderly manner. That way we can ensure that we maximize the value for the company. However, if the judge does not grant my motion, we must be ready to move with a viable alternative. Since Venture Funding doesn't hold liens on all of the company's assets, especially the cash and receivables, we may be able to gain the upper hand at the auction. But that will take an Oscar winning performance."

"What are our other options?" Peter asked. "I don't want to be down to only one course of action."

"I agree," Megan responded. "Tomorrow you will go and meet Martin Ivey in Galveston. If you can cut a deal, that will strengthen my hand before the judge. With a favorable ruling, then that will be our primary course of action. If he doesn't want the company, they we will need to grab all of the cash in the company using Stuart and Valerie's powers of attorney."

"What will that involve?" Peter inquired. "We are really down to the wire at that point."

"Let's look at the ownership of the company. You have 49%, Valerie has 41% and Stuart owns 10%. If the auction is held successfully on Friday, you will lose your stock, but the family will still control the company."

"Then will be lost."

"We are up against a formidable opponent. He has several months head start on us. I think you need to admit, there is no win-win option in this transaction. At best all we want to do is maximize the amount of cash we pull out of the company. That will provide security to Valerie and Stuart and give you some cash to start fresh. Besides, some fresh cash in your pocket might even give you the balls to ask me to marry you."

Peter was stunned by Megan's words. He never expected her to broach the subject of marriage. A few days ago, it seemed their relationship was permanently and irreparably damaged.

As Peter struggled with his response, Megan continued. "TMS owes a total of twenty-two million dollars on the bank loan now held by Venture Funding. The real estate and rolling stock are probably worth eighteen million dollars. The remainder of the other crap at the terminal is worth another one million to two million dollars, but that's at the top end. That leaves about two million dollars to extinguish the loan in total. If we can get the loan paid in full, then you can walk away from your guaranty. Otherwise, I can assure you McAdams will come after you for any deficiency."

"You don't think I have the balls to ask for your hand in marriage?" Peter asked.

"Don't change the subject. I'm on a roll," Megan cautioned. "They also have lien on company cash about one and one-quarter million dollars, but there are no restrictions as to its use under the loan documents. That leaves a seven hundred fifty thousand dollar gap. Therefore, the bids at the auction will be critical and we can be assured that McAdams' tact will be to under bid everything. He wants the maximum deficiency so he can tie you up in court thereby preventing you from contesting the sale. As far as that bastard Elmore is concerned, he's the wildcard. He, more than anyone, holds the potential to thoroughly trash our plans."

Peter thought for a few minutes. "We know about the error in the bank's collateral documents. Do you think they know about it in Chicago?" Peter asked. "Our game plan sounds far too simplistic to be successful. The logic flows but I think we need to anticipate what his move will be if he knows. Although your paralegal missed it, I'm not sure the attorney in Chicago did."

"Maybe he knows about it but thinks it isn't critical. Remember we are dealing with folks from Chicago. It is generally accepted that Texas laws can be confusing to out of state attorneys."

"I want to talk about this marriage thing," Peter interjected. "You're not waving me off."

"I'm not ready," Megan shot back. "We have plenty of issues to discuss."

Megan and Peter continued for several hours discussing various scenarios for the auction scheduled to occur in less than eighteen hours. Peter focused on the potential impact of Elmore's plans for the auction. "After what you said and knowing that Elmore is working with McAdams, I'm very concerned that the bids at the auction will definitely not payoff the loan. If Elmore wants to screw his partner, he may just as likely underbid," Peter suggested.

Megan screamed as she jumped to her feet, "Shit! That's that bastard's plan. And that is the worst outcome that could happen!"

"Explain!"

"McAdams thinks he is going into the deal with a buyer to pay somewhere slightly south of twenty-two million dollars to make the auction legitimate yet leave him some debt to chase you. In all likelihood the two of them even have a side deal where Elmore pays a premium to Venture Funding after the auction. That's his upside in the deal and he gets to double dip if he collects anything on your deficiency. What he doesn't know is that Elmore isn't on board and if as I now suspect he bids substantially less that the balance owing on the loan, you are royally screwed. Elmore then screws McAdams by not paying on the side promise. If he bids materially less, you will have to go into bankruptcy."

"I don't like what I am hearing. But wouldn't McAdams and Elmore have a formal side agreement on the premium to ensure Elmore pays up?"

"Certainly not!" Megan shouted as she retrieved additional documents from her briefcase. "If a side document did exist and it was later discovered, then they would be looking at jail time. You can't negotiate a preset price ahead of an auction in Texas. Even his high priced attorneys in Chicago know this. To win this battle, we will have to play out their cards in perfect sequence."

"What is our next step?" Peter asked.

"Are we ready to deal with Woody?" Megan asked. "I feel we need to feel him out and see if he tells us anything."

Megan's willingness to approach Woody excited Peter. He was ready to kick some Coppell ass. "I agree we need to confront him. Since we now agree he is dirty, I think we can take him on."

"Then we should meet with Woody first thing in the morning and advise him that we are throwing in the towel. If he is dirty, he will immediately call Chicago and maybe McAdams might drop his guard at the auction. All we need is for McAdams to be slightly off his game at the auction and not expect us to make a move."

Peter liked Megan's plan but had some concerns over timing. "But if we wait until tomorrow to confront Woody, then he may not have time to make the contact. McAdams will probably be in the air. And when he does speak to him, he may be too married to his strategy to drop his guard."

"Agreed."

"Call him now!"

CHAPTER 17

The phone rang almost eight times before Woody finally answered at his home. "It's after midnight," he complained passionately after glancing at caller ID. "What do you need?"

Peter pressed the speakerphone button and returned the receiver to its cradle. "Megan and I have been here for hours trying to devise a workable solution to get us out of this predicament in one piece; however, each time I roll the dice, I come up with snake eyes. Time is running out and we are agreed that we are facing a dead end."

"Have you finalized your strategy for the auction tomorrow?" Woody asked in a casual tone. "Are you even going to show up?"

"We are still debating whether we should even show up. Both of us don't want to witness the dismembering of the business. I think it's worse emotionally for all of us if we are there and can't do anything to stop the auction. But at the same time, I feel bad for the staff if we don't at least make an appearance."

"Have you talked to Stuart and Valerie? Do you think they would be willing to step up to the plate and provide some financial support to enable you to make an end run at the auction?"

"I spoke to both of them earlier this evening. You already know how those two feel about the company. They want nothing to do with it and are absolutely unwilling to put out a dime to save it. Besides, the money required to purchase the company at auction is too large without a major bank providing funding for the lion's share of the cost. At this late hour, that isn't going to happen."

Megan spoke up. "If only one of the banks can give us a commitment by tomorrow morning, I can find a judge to issue a temporary stay to stop the auction." She pressed the mute button and looked at Peter. "Let's see how he responds to the bank play."

Woody responded immediately. "It's a crying shame that the banks won't come through with the necessary financing to save TMS. I just knew we had a shot with them when I spoke to them on Tuesday. But now we have nothing."

Peter released the mute button on the phone. "What are you talking about?" Peter asked with a little edge in his voice. "The banks have made their decisions and you haven't told me. We had an agreement that you would call me the instant you heard anything from any of the banks."

"I guess it slipped my mind. Both John Bailey and Dave Fields called me late this afternoon. They reported that both banks are unwilling to loan you the money you need to refinance the Venture Funding loan. You were in Dallas and I didn't want to interrupt your meeting with Elmore. I expected you to call later and I planned tell you then. Besides if a sale was going to happen with Elmore, then bank financing isn't needed."

Peter pressed the mute button on the phone once again. He looked at Megan and saw anger building across her face. Her emotions boiled over. "That fucking bastard!" she screamed. "He's going to lie to us to the very end. I'm not taking this any more." She reached to release the mute button but Peter grabbed his arm.

"Calm down. Keep your evil twin in check. Remember we need information from him before we blow him away."

"You're right. I'm acting like you more and more," she said with a smile. "Keep him on the line and see what he will tell us."

Peter released the mute button and resumed his conversation with Woody. "Did they give any reasons for their decisions?" Peter asked calmly. "You were so certain that they would jump at the chance to get our business."

"The word is out on the street that the situation at the terminal is going to blow wide open and banks simply don't like to get involved in sticky deals. They have been spooked by the prospect of the auction tomorrow. Both liked what we outlined in the presentation and indicated that if you can somehow survive the auction, they will step up and advance whatever you need next week at the earliest."

"Clearly too little too late, but then that is all you can expect from banks today. Thanks anyway for your hard work these past few days. I couldn't have survived without you."

"That's what I'm here for," Woody replied in a near jovial tone. "You can always count on me. So what is your next step if may ask?"

Megan took the question. "I have explored all possible angles over the past three days. There is no way out for Peter and his family. I believe we cannot stop the auction and I have recommended to Peter that he throw in the towel. The decision for him has been difficult and I believe he is now ready to walk away and start fresh with another opportunity. He has enough seed money and with some outside investors can be up and running in a few months with a new business venture, hopefully one outside of the trucking industry."

The total capitulation by Peter and Megan surprised Woody. He was certain Peter would fight to the end and then take Union Bank and Marler McAdams to court before the start of the auction. It was totally out of character, especially for Megan to give up without one last push. He decided to probe for as much information as the pair was willing to release. "Are Stuart and Valerie okay with this approach?"

Peter moved near the phone and sighed heavily. "As hard as I tried, I couldn't convince them to help me save the company. Since they are unwilling to put up any money and they represent over half of the company, they fully understand the consequences of their inaction."

Megan broke into the conversation. "Peter spoke to both earlier and they are ready to walk away also. And as you well know, Valerie walked away years ago."

Woody did not say anything for several minutes. Peter and Megan did not want to break the agonizing silence. They threw out the bait and they desperately wanted him to swallow it then run out the line until he was solidly hooked. Once he had it solidly in his lip, they would reel him in.

After an inordinate amount of time, Woody restarted the conversation. "I'm sorry to hear the news. It's the finality of the decision that takes my breath away. If Megan says that there is no way out, then I have to believe it's the death nail. If she can't find a way, then it doesn't exist. Looks like I will need to start looking for a new job first thing in the morning. Have you thought about what you would like to do next?" he asked Peter.

"I haven't had the time to sit back and think about what I want to do next. I think I'll take some time off and maybe go to the lake. Bait some hooks and recharge my batteries. I'm not thinking clearly right now."

"After all the years you dedicated to running TMS, you deserve time off. You have squirreled some money away. Break it out and live a little."

Megan sensed that Woody accepted that all was hopeless for Peter and now was the right time to strike. She pressed the mute button and whispered to Peter. "Tug on the line and check to see if he's hooked. Listen to him brag. He thinks he's in the catbird seat."

Peter smiled as he released the mute button and addressed Woody with his voice breaking. "Megan wants me to call John Bailey and Dave Fields tomorrow morning to thank them for their efforts. They may be willing to finance my next business venture. After I get back from the lake, maybe you and I can get together and come up with a business proposal to float to the banks around town. I want to be well out in front of the curve and not stuck behind the eight ball again when I'm ready to move. This lesson has really taught me the critical importance of a reliable bank relationship."

The conversation was heading in a direction that Woody didn't want to follow. He stumbled with his response, but decided to make a clean split from Peter. "Thanks for the offer. I need to focus on my next opportunity. Maybe it is time for me to strike out on my own. Don't misunderstand what I'm about to say, but I think it is time for me to come out from behind your shadow."

"There is no question that this nightmare has impacted us all and we now need to rethink everything. I know Megan and I certainly have." Peter said in a reassuring voice. "We all must do what we believe is right for us. So, come out of my shadow and give me the telephone numbers for the banks. I will call them tomorrow while I am sitting around the house doing nothing."

"I'll have to look them up and get back to you," Woody responded. "If I were you, I think I would wait a few weeks before I call the banks. Let everything cool down."

"I don't want to wait. Besides, my calendar is wide open at this point. Megan just handed me something to write on, so give me their telephone numbers."

"I told you I need to look them up," Woody responded with a hint of belligerence. "I'll call you on Monday."

"I don't understand why you have to look up the numbers. I would think that since you have called them several times in the past couple of days, you would have them both stored in your short term memory."

"What are you implying that I have some ulterior motive for not giving you the numbers?" Woody asked with a gruff tone. "I've been working my ass off these past few days."

"I am firmly convinced that you have been working your ass off the past several months," Peter snorted. "You don't have the numbers for Fields and Bailey because you haven't spoken to them in months."

"If you think you know something, put it on the table," Woody chirped back. "Have you been checking on me behind my back?"

"Until I met with Elmore, I didn't think I had to. Now that you've asked, yes I did check on you. I spoke to both banks earlier today and I confirmed with Heather that you never sent anything out to them earlier in the week," Peter responded challenging all of Woody's earlier assertions. "You have been working hard these last few weeks, but for whom?"

"Okay," Woody confessed in a conciliatory tone. "The information can't help you at this juncture. It is true that I have been working against you these past several months."

"Months! I should have suspected that McAdams had someone on the inside to feed him information and short circuit our efforts."

"Marler McAdams!" Woody laughed. "You think I'm working for Marler McAdams?"

"If you're not working for McAdams, then who are you working for?"

"Phillip Elmore."

Peter and Megan simultaneously pressed the mute button. They looked at one another in total shock and surprise but said nothing. After about thirty seconds, Woody called out to see if the two were still on the phone. Peter released the mute button. "Phillip Elmore! How did you hook up with him?" Peter demanded. "I didn't see that one coming."

"I got a better offer and I took it. After the sale I will be in your office running TMS as a division of Dallas Metro," Woody disclosed with a loud laugh.

Megan once more hit the mute button and looked at Peter. He was moving his head from side to side in disbelief. She signaled for a response, but he had none. She wanted to know more about the opposition, but really didn't know what at ask. Why would Woody disclose any factual information about McAdams' and Elmore's intentions at the auction? In Dallas, Elmore revealed that he and McAdams were a team. Now that Woody saw himself in a position of safety, he just might reveal more than he should about his partner. Megan again released the mute button on the phone and questioned Woody further.

"I must admit that you certainly backed the right horse in this race," she said stroking his growing ego. "I don't understand how Elmore got invited to the table. From the start this quagmire looked like it was strictly a Marler McAdams orchestrated three ring circus."

"Marler McAdams doesn't know his ass from a hole in the ground," Woody asserted. "He's up in Chicago and thinks of himself as the grand marshal."

Megan smiled at Peter and whispered, "The bastard's hooked good and deep! Jerk hard on the line and reel him in!"

Peter wanted confirmation of what Elmore told him in Dallas. He cleared his throat and challenged Woody's assertions. "I can't believe that you're a player in this transaction. You're along for the ride and nothing else. I don't suspect for an instant that you know what McAdams and Elmore are planning for tomorrow."

Woody could not contain his temper. "I'm integral to this deal. When McAdams and Deutsch cooked up this foreclosure party for you guys months ago, they needed a legitimate company to come in as a viable bidder at the auction. Otherwise the auction could be challenged in court. Through his vast network of contacts, McAdams found Elmore and approached him with the proposal. Naturally, he took the bait. After all, he wanted TMS. The plan is for Elmore to slightly underbid the loan balance at the auction to create a deficiency with which to tie you up in court for the foreseeable future. McAdams worked out a prearranged bid pattern with a side agreement whereby Dallas Metro pays Venture Funding a premium for TMS after the auction."

"So Elmore is paying full value for TMS," Peter interjected. "I can't imagine that he is happy about that deal."

"Not in the least bit. Once Elmore recognized that he was getting screwed on this deal then he decided to shove it to McAdams in the shorts. McAdams' needs a quick auction to avoid any problems. He has already instructed the auctioneer to move through the auction process quickly tomorrow and not stop for anything. He doesn't want any delays whatsoever. What McAdams doesn't yet realize is that the auction will happen so fast that he will not have any time to react or stop the process."

Peter responded to Woody revelations. "That is a great plan. McAdams does believe he is in total control. That's his standard position, absolute control."

"And that will be his downfall," Woody cracked with a laugh.

"How did you get pulled into this deal?" Peter inquired. He wanted to know everything, and as long as Woody was willing to talk, he and Megan were willing to listen and probe for as much as they could get.

"In the office the other day, I told you that I knew Elmore's CFO. They gave me a call and offered me a sweet proposal. I grabbed it. Best part is that McAdams doesn't know he's being tooled."

Peter had enough. He uncorked the bottle and released all of the pent up pressure, "You're fired you ungrateful bastard!"

Woody did not waste a second in responding to Peter's action. "That's fine with me. I won't need to clean out my desk. All I will have to do on Monday is move my shit into your office."

"Do not set foot at TMS again," Peter instructed. "I'm calling security at the terminal." With those last words, Peter picked up the receiver and slammed it back into its cradle immediately disconnecting the call. He exhaled heavily, then picked it up again and called the security station at the terminal and barked his orders. "Woody Coppell has been fired. Do not let him on the premises under any circumstances."

Megan sat back in her chair and exhaled loudly. "I never saw that one coming. Of all the people that could have been working against us, this just surprises the crap out of me."

"That's the problem. It is always the ones you never suspect. They are successful because you never question what they do. After this incident, I will never let that happen to me again."

"I find it interesting that Woody was working with Elmore and not McAdams. The Deutsch-McAdams link is understandable, but…"

Peter sat up in his chair. Simultaneously, he and Megan hit on the same thought. Peter struggled to convert his thoughts into coherent words for the both of them. "If Woody is working for Elmore and Deutsch is working for McAdams, then…"

Megan screamed, "Who the fuck at TMS is working for McAdams? That bastard wouldn't work a deal of this size totally blind!"

CHAPTER 18

"Do you have any idea what time it is?" Elmore asked the caller with his usual gruffness. "I need my rest so that I will be thinking clearly at the auction tomorrow afternoon. This better be important."

"You might want to know that Peter Ferrell and his bitch are throwing in the towel. I just got off the phone with the two of them. They can't figure out a viable way to stop the auction sale."

"Can you trust them or could it be a ploy to get us to drop our guard?"

"They sounded sincere on the phone. Neither his mother nor his uncle is willing to come to the table with cash to bail him out. Without a bank to refinance the deal, they are out of options. Now that they know that I was sabotaging their efforts, there is no way for them to recover with less than a day remaining before the auction."

"We suspected that Ferrell might uncover your inaction with the banks if he bothered to check it out. Frankly, I'm surprised it took him this long to make the call. How much did you tell them?" Elmore asked with a hint of concern building in his voice. "I trust you didn't go too far and tell them everything."

"That information can't hurt you now. Time is out and they have no place to turn."

"You are a miserable worthless fool Woody! You told them everything didn't you?" Elmore screamed, as Woody remained silent. "Why did you allow your ego to get the better of you? You represented to me from the start that you were a rock solid professional who could keep his head clear when the going got tough. Here we are on the cusp of hitting the jackpot and you come down with a severe case of diarrhea of the mouth. If you screw this up for me, there will be no place for you to hide."

JIM ARDOIN

"Calm down you worry wart," Woody shot back with firmness in his voice. "I told them because Ferrell thought I was working for McAdams."

"What's the value of that information?" Elmore responded. "You're a piss ant snitch; it's irrelevant that they know you don't work for McAdams."

"You're a stupid fool," Woody asserted. "For all of your bravado, you're just a two bit redneck trucker to the core."

"Don't go too far Coppell!" Elmore warned. "I haven't paid you yet and I'm starting to feel that any expenditure at this point is a waste."

"For a good part of the week, Ferrell and Cedars have been thinking that there was someone on the inside working with McAdams against them. After he called the banks and discovered that I was the snitch, they have been patting themselves on the back. Their earlier call was a ploy to find out what I knew. Why else would they call at midnight? That's Deutsch's trick."

"So what's your point?" Elmore demanded with his anger still boiling. "I'm getting tired of all of this cloak and dagger shit."

"My point is this. Those two are now racking their brains trying to determine who is working for McAdams on the inside. They were so fucking convinced that I was the spy that they stopped looking. So between now and the auction, they are going to spend every waking minute looking for McAdams' mole. When you get to the auction, the game will be under your total and complete control."

"Well played Coppell. I guess you've earned your money after all. McAdams will never see the freight train barreling his direction until after he's a grease spot on the tracks."

※※※

"You think you know someone then they do the unexpected," Peter lamented to Megan.

"I thought I knew Woody as well as anyone could. This was not something I would have ever expected him to do," Megan responded. "To make matters worse, I never doubted Woody because I didn't think he had the moxie to do this."

"I wasn't talking about Woody," Peter said flashing a grin across his face.

"I don't know what you mean," Megan said softly with her eyes looking away from Peter.

"What changed your mind?" Peter asked calmly. He didn't want to let his nasty genie out of the bottle. "I thought we were done for good after our fight the other night."

Megan drew in then exhaled a deep breath. It was time for her to come clean with Peter. Their relationship demanded clarification before they could move forward to the next level. "The other night I was angry because you wear your hot temper on your sleeve ready to turn loose at the slightest provocation. That aspect of your personality has always angered me."

Peter started to respond, but she held up her hand signaling for him to keep his silence. "My whole life has been that of a supporting character. I never learned how to successfully engage in the sorts of confrontations that you must effectively deal with on a daily basis. Since I am a corporate attorney, I always remain completely and securely detached from the business transactions. Rarely do I see my clients tear one another to shreds. The only exception involves you and TMS. Unfortunately, because of our personal relationship, I have been drawn into the fire on this McAdams thing. Frankly, I don't know how you do it day in and day out. I see now that if you didn't there would be no business. The twists and turns over these past four days have allowed me to see the whole picture. I realize that our relationship can survive, but only if we work together to keep it separate from the business transactions."

Peter moved next to Megan and rested his hands on hers. "I don't know what to say..." he started. "I have been a complete fool."

"We have both been complete fools."

"So there is nothing more that we need to say to one another at this juncture in our relationship?" Peter asked.

"Just one thing more," Megan whispered. "I want it to be permanent."

Peter looked at Megan and spoke softly, "I love you."

"I know."

The couple continued their discussions for another half hour then decided it was getting late. The next eighteen hours would be the most important hours of their lives. Before they retired for the night, Megan brought up a few final items. She reached for her leather briefcase and removed several documents. "Here are powers of attorney we need from your mother and uncle. This allows us to do whatever is necessary as the owners of the company. Whatever we do tomorrow, it is absolutely critical that we follow the letter of the law. I don't want to give McAdams or Elmore any loose ends to sue us on in the coming weeks and potentially unravel whatever we decide to do. The auction must clean the decks completely."

"I will swing by on my way to work in the morning to get their signatures. At the office, I will call Ivey. By the way, have you heard anything regarding Cleveland?"

Megan waved a second document. "Yes, the investigator called today and faxed me this preliminary report. He promised to have a final more detailed report to me early tomorrow."

"Did he find anything, anything at all?"

"It seems Deutsch pulled the same thing in Cleveland about two years ago and the results were bad."

"Was McAdams involved?" Peter asked anxiously.

"He was in it up to his neck."

Peter smiled. "That's wonderful news!"

"I thought you would like it."

Megan's tone changed and she moved close to Peter. She hesitated briefly before she started. She did not want to understate the seriousness of her message. "When Deutsch first told us about the sale of the loan to Venture Funding, I though this was going to be a cake walk to find a favorable resolution. But I'm concerned that there are too many people working against us and you are going to lose everything."

As tears started to stream from Megan's eyes, Peter raised his hand to stop her from saying anything further. "Everything will be fine. Don't worry."

"That's what I'm trying to tell you. It's not going to be fine," Megan confided with a sorrowful look. "This is far harder than I thought. I let you down. I should have insisted that you hire another lawyer to handle this matter. I'm not that good with this sort of thing. You needed a street fighter, someone who is willing to get down in the dirt and scratch and claw for every inch of ground." Megan stood and moved near the window.

"I need you and only you. Together we will get through this and laugh all the way to the bank. Sure we are going to get some cuts and scrapes tomorrow, and will probably spill some blood. But I'm telling you the other guys will come out looking much worse."

Megan hung her head. "Peter it's over."

Peter bolted from the couch, grabbed Megan and shook her. "This goddamn three ring circus isn't over until I say it's over. In business we fight until there is no more fight in us then we throw some more punches. You never give up."

"I don't understand how you keep going. Clearly it's a lost cause at this point, walk away."

"You keep going because that is what life is about. When you stop you die. These bastards picked with wrong pair to go after. Tomorrow evening McAdams will go back to Chicago knowing that he was in the fight of his life. He sure as shootin' won't be coming back to Houston anytime soon."

Megan laughed under her breath. "I'll keep working but I still think it's a lost cause."

"Let me decide when we throw up our hands and walk away."

"Then we are lost for sure," Megan said with a sneer. "If we don't call it a day and get some sleep, there will be no point in going to bed at all."

"There are plenty of things we can do in bed besides sleep."

At exactly one fifty, the phone on Peter's night table sprang to life. Peter picked up the receiver and answered the phone. "This is Peter Ferrell."

"This is Mike Turner at the terminal. I hate to bother you but some folks just showed up and they are acting as if they owned the place. They are saying something about an auction scheduled for tomorrow and we cannot stop their activities. What do you want me to do?" Mike related with anxiety flowing through his every word.

"Call the police and I will be there in a half hour."

"What's going on?" Megan asked concerned over the nature of the call.

"It was Mike at the terminal. McAdams' auction company has showed up and wants to take control of the yard and set up for the auction."

Megan knew the law and immediately offered advice. "They can't do anything until five o'clock tomorrow. That is when we are in final default. I'll get dressed and go with you."

Peter was already halfway to the closet. He stopped and issued his orders to Megan. "No. Stay here. I will call you if I need you."

It was about a half hour after the call when Peter screamed into the terminal in Megan's BMW. What he found upon his arrival was not at all what he anticipated. The terminal was a scene of total confusion. He parked the car where he stopped and walked over to where Mike Turner had assembled a large contingent of TMS drivers and terminal workers. "What's going on," he asked. "I'm not in the mood for this tonight."

Mike pointed to about a dozen individuals who stood just inside the terminal gate. "They arrived about a half hour ago and started to take charge. When they wouldn't stop, I got the men together and we moved them to the entrance. After I called you, I called the police. What do you want to do?" he asked.

After assessing the situation, Peter barked his orders. "Get them out of here immediately."

No sooner had the words left Peter's lips when a sheriff's constable from Harris County, Texas arrived with his lights flashing. He exited the cruiser and stepped up to Peter. "Who is in charge here," he demanded as he barked his location into the communication device attached to the left epaulet on his shirt.

Peter stepped forward and responded. "I'm Peter Ferrell the

owner and these gentlemen have no business here. They are trespassing and I want them removed from the premises immediately."

The constable walked toward the auction representatives with Peter and Mike less than a few steps behind. The constable repeated his request. "Who is in charge?"

One of the auctioneers stepped forward and handed the constable a letter. He removed his flashlight from his belt and flashed it on the letter. He read aloud its contents so that everyone assembled near the gate to the terminal could hear. "This is a letter from a Marler McAdams instructing San Jacinto Auctioneers to conduct an auction on Friday evening exactly at five o'clock and to do whatever preparation is necessary to facilitate a quick sale." The deputy turned to Peter and said, "What do you have to say about this."

Peter struggled to keep his composure. "They have every right to come onto the property tomorrow after five o'clock. They have absolutely no right to be here until then. If you like I will call my lawyer and she can confirm what I am telling you."

He handed the letter to the auction team. "Looks like you boys need to leave and not return until five tomorrow."

Suddenly, pushing and shoving erupted between the two groups. Next, fists flew. Several of the men fell to the ground pounding one another with their fists. Finally, the constable stepped in and threatened to arrest everyone if another blow landed on its mark. Reluctantly, the auction team got into their vehicles and departed. Peter thanked the constable.

He turned and addressed Mike. "Has all of the rolling stock returned to the terminal?"

"They are expected to be here by no later than noon."

"Listen. It is going to be hectic around here tomorrow. I want you to keep everyone around until the auction is over. Tell them they will be paid an extra four hours to stay. After the auction, there will be some important announcements."

CHAPTER 19

Peter glanced at his watch as he pulled Megan's convertible into his garage. It was a little past four thirty in the morning. The unending avalanche of problems ensured that he would get no sleep before the auction. He tipped toed into the bedroom and found Megan fast asleep. The noise of a shower would no doubt awake Megan so Peter decided to get undressed and grab a few winks without a shower.

As he neared the bed, Megan groaned softly then turned in Peter's direction. She sat up slightly and spoke Peter. "Did you get it all straightened at the terminal?"

Peter finished undressing and rolled into the bed. He moved near Megan and said, "McAdams' goons left after the constable arrived."

"You could have called me."

"I know but I wanted you to get some sleep so at least one of us would be worth a damn today."

Megan reached for the clock on the table and moaned. The alarm would sound in less than an hour. "Since there is no point in trying to catch some sleep in the next hour, do you want to snuggle?" Megan asked throwing back the covers to reveal that she was wearing only her thong.

"I would love to. But right now, I am so tired that I couldn't give you the attention you deserve."

"Well, just lay back and I will take of everything," she purred. "I rarely get the opportunity to be on top."

Peter chuckled. "You are always on top in case you haven't noticed."

"I'm talking about in bed, not business."

"I've been thinking," Peter said as Megan threw back the bedcovers and removed her delicate thong. She got up on her knees and moved toward the head of the bed. There she reached up and grabbed the headboard with both hands, pulling herself forward. Next she extended her long shapely leg across Peter's muscular torso. The distinctive fragrance of raw sexuality wafted above Peter's face. He found the smell intoxicating. Megan shifted her weight and slowly sat down high on his chest. His physical reaction was instantaneously. She then slowly slid her body down his, grinding from side to side until she was resting on his lower stomach. "Let's fly to Las Vegas after the auction. I want a change of scenery," Peter insisted, his words breaking as he struggled to breathe.

"What are we going to do in Las Vegas?" Megan asked. "All they have in Vegas is gambling, and after throwing the dice this week, I've had enough risk taking to last me a lifetime."

"We could get a big suite at the Bellagio and spend as long as we can in bed. See some shows and hit the best restaurants."

"Sounds boring," Megan complained in a whining tone. "I want excitement."

"Then we could get married," Peter said as he reached up and caressed Megan as she rhythmically rubbed her supple body against his torso.

"The first step in the marriage dance is to ask for my hand in marriage. I don't remember you ever asking me to marry you," Megan stated casually. "I want a little romance with my uninhibited sex."

Peter moaned in response to Megan gyrations. "Ask you missy? I believe you did the asking earlier and I graciously accepted."

"I don't remember that, but I'm willing to do whatever my little baby wants," Megan replied as she leaned forward and kissed Peter on the chest. As she did, her body slid further down his torso. "Oh my god," she nearly screamed as she reached behind and stroked Peter. "See, I knew you weren't that tired. I can work with this."

At five o'clock, Peter's alarm clock sprang to life with its annoying shrill. The couple failed to turn off the alarm when they decided to engage in a little extracurricular activity. Megan was closest to the clock so she reached over and turned it off. "I'm going to take a shower," she advised Peter. "Care to join me?"

"If we are going to get an early start to this wretched day, I better just get to the kitchen and start the coffee. If you are still in the shower when I'm done, I'll join you."

In the kitchen Peter quickly completed his chores then stepped outside to retrieve the morning paper. When he returned to the house with the morning paper, he heard the water in the shower stop. He grabbed a cup of coffee, opened the paper and sat at the table. After he had read a few pages, Megan stepped into the kitchen wearing a long white terrycloth robe. She retrieved a mug from the cabinet and poured it full with black coffee. She walked around the table, leaned over and kissed Peter firmly on the lips. He reached inside the robe, grabbed her bottom and pulled her close. She pulled away and warned, "I don't have time for any more loving. I need to prepare for the court hearing."

Peter released his hold and returned to his reading. He looked up and watched as Megan walked out of the kitchen carrying her cup of coffee. Before he finished the paper, Megan was back in the kitchen fully dressed and carrying the empty mug. She placed it in the sink and sat at the table. "Are we both square on our schedules today? We can't have a misstep on anything if we are to be successful."

"Don't worry," Peter insisted. "Everything will go off without a hitch. Trust me."

"Trust you. We both know you are lying through your teeth. Nothing is going to go right for us today," Megan whined. "It's the first rule of business."

"Nothing's fair. That's why there are lawyers."

Within a half hour of Megan's departure, Peter stepped out of the front door. It was a cloudless day and a light breeze blew in from the Gulf. "The calm before the storm," he whispered under his breath. He walked across the wet grass in his front yard and once again climbed into the cab of his truck. Within seconds the big rig roared to life as Peter went tearing down the street. Peter opened his cell and called for Martin Ivey, but his phone went directly into voice messaging. He left a brief message telling Ivey that he will call him again in about an hour from the TMS terminal.

The terminal was silent when Peter arrived. No trucks were moving and most of the workers were standing around in groups talking. Peter parked his truck and entered the office. Immediately, Heather stepped forward and addressed Peter. "What is going on?" she cried in a panic. "Rumors are flying. Is the company going out of business?"

Peter didn't respond to Heather but rather he grasped her arm and directed her into his office. Once inside, he closed the door and told her to sit in one of the chairs facing his desk. "Over the last few days, we have been dealing with a serious situation with our bank. On Monday, they sold our loan to that outfit out of Chicago called Venture Funding. I'm not going to go into all of the details, but this afternoon at five o'clock, Venture Funding will conduct an auction of the assets of the company and effectively we will be out of business. I am still working to find a solution that will avoid the auction and allow everyone to keep working. But I must be honest and tell you that it is unlikely that I will be able to stop the auction."

"So what does it mean? Will I have a job or not?" Heather asked as she stood and moved near Peter's desk.

"I don't know what will happen with everyone's jobs. The new owner may continue to operate the terminal and keep everyone around. We are working to cause as little disruption as possible to the most of our workers. I know you have worked here for several years and..."

"I need this job. My boyfriend was laid off from his job yesterday afternoon. If I lose my job, then our marriage plans will be delayed."

"I appreciate your situation. I would like to be able to give you more, but I can't at this time," he said as he directed Heather from his office. "Please ask Bill Cobb to step into my office."

Before Heather left Peter's office she addressed her boss again. "Where's Woody? He is usually in by this time."

"Woody is no longer employed at TMS. Please get Bill."

With a look of total confusion, Heather slowly walked out of Peter's office. Within a few minutes, Bill Cobb walked in. "Heather said you wanted to see me," Cobb announced as he stepped into Peter's office. "Did you want me to bring you any financial information for your review?"

"Just close the door. I have some important information to share with you."

Cobb did as he was instructed then he sat down in front of Peter's desk. Over the next half hour, Peter updated Cobb on all of the developments since midnight Monday. The look of shock quickly crossed Cobb's face. "It doesn't surprise me that Woody screwed the company. I never liked the guy and only stayed around because of you and your father," Cobb confessed. "What do you need me to do?"

"Do not leave the office today for any reason and I need you at your desk and on-line with our bank."

After Cobb left the office Peter once again called Martin Ivey. This time he answered his phone. "Martin, this is Peter Ferrell with Transportation Management Services in Houston. My Uncle, Stuart Ferrell, suggested I give you a call to discuss a possible merger of our two companies."

"This is quite a surprise," Ivey revealed. "I don't know that I want to merge, but I certainly would discuss the acquisition of certain parts of your business. What is your timing?"

"I want to close immediately, in fact today if at all possible."

"Can you drive to Galveston so we can discuss this matter?"

"I can leave now and be there in a couple of hours. But I don't want to make the trip if you are not serious about getting a deal closed immediately."

"Let me call my bank and see if they can handle a large cash transfer. I'll get right back to you." Within five minutes, Ivey was back on the line. "I got the thumbs up from the bank. I will see you in two hours."

Peter immediately called Megan to give her the good news. "Ivey is interested. He has the funding available with his bank. I leave immediately to go to Galveston."

"I will draft the documents and leave the key business points blank so that the two of you can fill them in later," Megan advised.

"Do you have the signed powers of attorney from your mother and uncle?"

"Crap!" Peter screamed. "I left them on the kitchen table."

"There is no need to panic. I will send a runner to pick them up and get them signed."

"Don't bother. I will swing by the house on my way back from Galveston and get their signatures. How is everything going?" Peter asked.

"After I draft the sale documents, I will walk to the courthouse for the hearing. I will call you if anything develops."

"Hopefully the hearing will give us the breathing room we need."

Peter pulled out of the TMS terminal at exactly eight thirty.

CHAPTER 20

The traffic on Interstate 45 between Houston and Galveston was unusually heavy, even for a Friday morning. Peter arrived at Coastal Truckers on the East end of Galveston Island at ten forty-five. Ivey stepped out of the office and greeted Peter as he stepped down from his truck. "You made good time getting here. I know you are in a rush so let's step inside to my office and get started."

"That's exactly what I wanted to hear," Peter revealed breathing a huge sigh of relief. "I have had a difficult couple of days."

As the two men walked to Coastal's offices, Peter looked around the terminal and was pleased to see that it was a first class operation. Like TMS, neatness and order were evident throughout the yard. Inside Coastal's offices, Peter revealed everything to Ivey. By this juncture he believed he had nothing to lose. If this was another wild goose chase, then it was Stuart Ferrell who made the error by referring his nephew to Ivey. "I realize that this is a considerable volume of information to absorb at one sitting, but I wanted you to have all of the facts."

Ivey sat back in his chair. "Over the years, I have heard more than enough negative things about Phil Elmore and Dallas Metro. Your statements confirm that he is someone to avoid at all costs. Tell me, how is my old friend Stuart doing? I was really disappointed when he retired. He is one damn good Gin Rummy player. Years ago he would invite me to these great duck hunts in Anahuac. At first I thought he just wanted me to do more business with TMS. Over time I learned that all he wanted to do was sit me down at the card table and separate me from my money. I know that you didn't drive to Galveston to talk about the past. You are here to discuss business."

Peter took a deep breath and then released it slowly. He was about to make the most important sales pitch of his life. "I am here to offer TMS for sale."

"I'd like to help you but I don't need all of TMS."

The news surprised Peter. He sat up in his seat and quickly challenged Ivey. "What do you want?"

The message from Ivey was clean and clear. "All I need is the delivery contracts. I have considerable idle rolling stock and want to expand. If you are willing to only sell the contracts, then we have a deal. I would also take your staff in Houston and reopen a shuttered facility I own there. I believe it is about two miles from TMS. If I understand your situation, my offer might work."

Peter was surprised by Ivey the specifics of Ivey's offer. "How do you know about the particulars of my situation?"

Ivey leaned back in the chair and laughed. "You don't know your uncle very well do you? He called me late last night at home to pre-grease this meeting. He said he didn't need you running down another box canyon, whatever that means."

Peter shook his head and laughed to himself. "I am learning a great deal more about my family with each passing day," Peter confessed. "Your deal sounds like it might be workable. Do you mind if I call my attorney?"

"I will step out so you can talk to her in private."

As Ivey walked from the office, Peter opened his cell and quickly called Megan's number. "Ivey says that he only wants the contracts. He doesn't need the whole ball of wax. Where do we stand on the motion?" Peter asked with his impatience intermingled with his words.

"I am almost to the courthouse. Since we hold the contracts free and clear, a sale of them on a stand-alone basis really works. Cut your deal and get back. If I get the stay, then we can re-cut the deal as needed. I don't want you to be late to the auction."

Peter stood and opened the door to Ivey's office. He stepped out and looked down the hall. He did not see anyone in either direction, but then he heard Ivey's voice echoing from down the hall. With timid steps he walked toward the sound of Ivey's voice. Several offices down the hall he found Coastal's owner leaning over a desk reviewing a stack of financial reports. Ivey caught Peter's shadow moving across the floor and stepped from behind the desk. "All done?" he asked with a smile. "What's the price?"

Peter did not immediately reply to Ivey's question. He was uncomfortable discussing the financial end of the deal in someone else's office. Ivey recognized Peter's hesitation and he let out a loud roar. "Don't worry. You can speak freely. This is my son Ray," Ivey disclosed as he pointed to the young man behind the desk. "He is the chief financial officer here at Coastal Truckers."

"Twelve million," Peter blurted out to the two men. "Twelve million dollars."

"Any room for negotiation," Ray asked. "In my experience there is always an appetite to accept less, especially to achieve a quick sale."

Peter laughed and responded to Ray comments. "Are you asking me to go duck hunting?"

The expression on Ray's face turned blank. Martin on the other hand again roared with laughter at Peter's comments. "Touché!"

"Ray, our family decided on a fair price for the contracts and we are not willing to negotiate."

"What assurances do we have that this deal doesn't get squashed post auction? I don't want to be at risk," Ray stated openly as he look at his father.

Martin rubbed his hand across his face. "The kids got a point."

Peter thought for a few seconds. He certainly did not want to return to Houston empty handed as he did the day before returning from Dallas. "We can close into escrow. Let a third party hold your money until the contracts are recorded. I will do whatever you want to protect you," Peter assured Ivey.

"I believe you. That won't be necessary. The Ferrell name means a great deal." Ivey looked at Ray who flashed a slight nod. "Is Stuart on board with this number?" he asked.

"In fact the number is his."

"Then we have a deal. What about documents?" Ivey asked. "If you want to move quickly we need to review them within the hour."

Suddenly, the cell phone on Peter's belt began to vibrate. It was Megan calling. He excused himself and returned to Ivey's office. As he walked into the office, he closed the door. "What do you need?" he asked still giddy after cutting the deal for the contracts.

In a full scream, Megan began her tirade. "I showed up at court here in Houston and we are not on the docket this afternoon. There will be no hearing on our motion! So we have no way to stop the auction!"

"I thought the court hearing was scheduled on the docket?"

"That's what I understood. Unfortunately my paralegal was bribed by none other than Marler McAdams and she didn't file my motion to stop the sale. She sat in my office and lied to my face that she did."

"So basically you are telling me we have nothing. We cannot stop the auction nor can we play a role in the bidding," Peter stated bitterly.

Still seething over the turn of events, Megan responded to Peter's statement. "We do have the sale of the contracts to Coastal. I will call Martin's attorney, fill in the blanks and e-mail the final documents for execution."

With their options quickly thinning, Peter pressed for all available information on the petition problem. "What did the bitch say when you confronted her with the facts?"

"Candidly, I was surprised she was still in the office when I returned from the courthouse. She was too stupid to leave. I can only assume that she thought she could send McAdams updates to the very end."

"What was her reason for doing it?" Peter asked.

"She did it for the oldest reason of all, cold hard cash. It seems that on McAdams' directions she intentionally didn't review the bank's documents. He wanted us in the dark. Therefore, he knew about the error and didn't want us to discover it. In speaking to her, it is clear that she doesn't know if he fully understands the implication of the error. He has relied on lawyers in Chicago to review the documents. She was just paid handsomely to impede our efforts."

"Then McAdams doesn't know what we are planning," Peter concluded sounding more upbeat.

"He's been trying to uncover our intentions. When Leslie told him about the petition I was preparing, he instructed her not to file it. Without our day in court, we have no way to stop the auction."

"What do you intend to do with Leslie?" Peter asked.

"I've already fired her skanky ass! That whore will never turn another trick in Houston!" Megan responded in a huff. "And damn it felt good!"

Peter laughed as he visualized a tremendous smile on Megan's face.

"So it's downhill from here," Megan said. "I told you it wouldn't work out in the end."

The sudden change in Megan tone caught Peter by surprise. "This is not the end. We have a full five hours remaining. Get the documents to Ivey and I will head back to Houston."

"Peter, I don't believe there is sufficient time to get documents reviewed, corrected, signed and funded," Megan stressed.

"You will get it closed," Peter insisted. "I haven't come this far to let it everything collapse because of a little paperwork. Sit down at your desk and get this done!"

Megan resisted and continued to plead her case. "There is no way that we can close today. I am telling you that there is not sufficient time. I can keep plugging away but we will come up short. Marler McAdams has won. We tried our best. What more do you want from me?"

The situation was spinning out of control. Without missing a beat, Peter stepped up to the plate and took control. "Calm down Megan," Peter stressed keeping his voice calm. "Take a deep breath. There is more than enough time. The men of TMS always make their deliveries on the mark. You've got McAdams and Elmore by the balls. Start squeezing! By the end of the auction, they will be eunuchs."

"When are you going to accept that right now it's your balls on the chopping block? There is not a fucking thing I can do to stop the hatchet from falling. You won't be shooting anything after the auction is over!"

Peter had enough and cut loose on his attorney. He held back nothing. "You have been berating me for years over the roughshod way I handle my business. Then when I need you to step up to the line and grab a hold of a tough situation, you crap out on me. Listen to me sister and listen damn good. I am in this deal to the very end and so are you. Pull your thumb out of your goddamn ass and put it in high gear. I'm not staying at the fucking Motel 6 in Vegas this weekend."

With nothing further to say to his attorney, Peter slammed the phone closed. He remained alone in Ivey's office a few minutes regaining his composure. He found the sudden release of all of his pent up anger to be reinvigorating. He had a new lease on life. After his breathing returned to normal he walked to Ray's office. He advised them to expect documents shortly and thanked the two for their willingness to help him out of an awful situation.

Outside Coastal's offices, Peter again called Megan. "Ivey and his attorney are waiting for the documents. He says his bank can make the transfer. You have my power of attorney so you can sign for TMS. So what is our next step?"

The earlier conversation was a wake-up call to Megan. Her tone was completely changed. "We will have to amend our approach, move to Plan C and if lady luck is riding our bumper it might work, maybe. The sale to Ivey must close in the next few hours or we are dead in the water."

"He claims he can close and fund today. I have no reason to doubt him," Peter said in his confident tone.

Megan's voice was measured and deliberate. "Both McAdams and Elmore believe they are in the driver's seat and that we have thrown in the towel."

"Also we have identified McAdams' mole. I am confident no more information will leak out to the opposition."

"They will never see us coming. Our chances are looking much better."

Megan laughed at Peter confidence. "We are going to the auction with nothing more than calluses on our hands from jerking this deal. And it will be down to the wire," Megan warned. "Don't forget about the two powers of attorney from Stuart and Valerie."

"I will swing by and drop off them off at your office once I have them."

"I don't need them until we meet at the terminal. Bring them to me there. On second thought, if you run late, just call me and tell me that they have been signed."

"I have a good feeling this may just work."

"I still don't know if we have enough time remaining. The bank wires close in a couple of hours."

Upon his return to Houston, Peter drove immediately to his home in Bellaire to retrieve the powers of attorney for his mother and uncle. He stepped out of the house with the documents and ran to his truck. When he turned the key, the time on the dash flashed two thirty-five. The auction was now less than two and a half hours away and his list of open items was still long as his arm. Time was not an ally. It was Friday afternoon and in the building traffic, Peter would be hard pressed to make his two stops and return to the TMS terminal on the northeast side of Houston by the start of the auction.

He called his uncle and told him he was running out of time and asked if he could meet him on the corner outside his condominium project to sign his power of attorney. Peter calculated that he did not have enough time to check through security and run up the elevator to Stuart's unit. Stuart agreed to the meeting.

When he arrived at the entrance to the complex, Stuart was waiting outside as he was instructed. Upon seeing Peter's truck, he rushed over and jumped in. He slammed the door closed and instructed Peter to continue driving. "Take me to your mother's house. She called earlier and asked me to drive her to the auction."

Stuart's news surprised Peter. He screamed at his uncle. "Mom wants to go to the auction?"

"She thinks it will bring closure for her and she will be able to get on with her life. I'm only doing what she asked. Now drive," he instructed pointing forward with his right index finger. "I thought you said you were pressed for time."

Peter stomped on the accelerator but soon he found himself deadlocked in traffic. Slowly he and Stuart crawled along San Felipe Road toward Tanglewood. Peter told Stuart of the deal he cut with Ivey as well as Megan's strategy for the auction."

Stuart leaned over and smiled. "I knew you could cut a deal with Martin. He owes me."

Peter laughed. "He told me that you called him to discuss the sale."

"I trust you aren't mad. But I've got my own interest to protect."

Stuart reached over and removed Peter's phone from his belt. "What are you doing?" Peter asked.

Stuart opened the Peter's cell and started punching numbers. "I'm calling your mother to meet us on the corner to sign her power of attorney. I don't want to delay you needlessly."

As Peter turned off San Felipe and onto Yorktown, he saw his mother standing on the next corner. He eased his truck to the curb and she jumped inside. Stuart had the document ready for her signature. After she signed, he placed the executed power of attorney in the large manila envelope along with his. With Megan's requirements completed, they both exited the truck.

"Where are you going?" Peter asked the pair. "You can ride to the terminal with me."

"No," Valerie responded. "Go on ahead by yourself. We will be there shortly."

Stuart walked around to the driver's window. He stood on the tips of his toes and whispered to Peter. "I'll tell your mother all about the deal on the way."

Peter again looked at his watch. It was already three fifty-seven. He was uncertain whether he could make the trip to the terminal in sixty-three minutes. To make matters worse, he held the critical documents that Megan needed

CHAPTER 21

As Peter drove down Breen Road toward TMS, he noticed a large number of vehicles parked along the shoulder of the road. Immediately, he realized it was the local gawkers gathering to watch the dismembering of TMS. They were like sharks moving in for the feast after having tasted the scent of blood in the water. He pulled into the terminal and noticed someone parked in his spot. It was a rental unit so Peter concluded that Marler McAdams helped himself to the best slot on the lot. With no other places available, Peter merely pulled his huge rig parallel to the curb and threw it into park.

Outside his vehicle, he scanned the facility. A crowd of about sixty had gathered and were milling about. None appeared to be legitimate buyers. Many were invited by the auctioneer to ensure the appearance of a lawful auction. By this time, all business at the terminal had ceased. Virtually every worker remained on the clock. Many were out on the pavement gathered in small groups. Peter observed that several in the group pointed in his direction as he stepped over to the office.

Suddenly, Peter heard someone blowing a car horn at the gate to the terminal. He turned to see Megan pulling into the terminal with her horn blaring to encourage several bystanders to move out of her way. Like Peter, she indiscriminately parked her car. She stepped out and joined Peter near the entrance to the office. Peter spoke first. "I think you are in a fire lane young lady," he mused.

"Let the bastards tow me," she quipped. "They will never be able to get into the lot. It's like a fucking circus around here. Do you have the signed powers of attorney?"

Peter handed Megan the large manila envelope containing the two executed documents.

"Let's get this show on the road," she instructed as she grabbed for the doorknob to the office.

"What's the latest on Ivey?" Peter inquired with a worried look starting to morph onto his face.

"He has all of the paperwork and instructions where to send funds for a good hour and a half," she said with a sigh as she looked at her watch. "If he wants the TMS contracts, this is his only opportunity. It was three minutes to five. Time is out."

"Don't worry; they never start exactly at the top of the hour."

She opened the front door wide and the two stepped inside the office. There in the reception area they found Marler McAdams in charge of all activity in the office. He barked his orders to the professional auctioneer he hired to commence the auction sale at once. In addition, McAdams also had at his side a Harris County Constable. It was clear he wanted no trouble and was not going to be stopped in his mission.

Peter stepped over to the constable with Megan in tow. "Let me make this perfectly clear. I own this company, not McAdams. He can't do anything until after the sale is complete and only if he is the successful bidder. I have my attorney here to answer any questions you might have. McAdams is from Chicago and is not familiar with the laws of the State of Texas. It does not appear that he brought his attorney from Chicago." Peter then turned to McAdams and in a challenging tone continued. "And I do not believe that Mr. McAdams is an attorney."

Megan stepped forward and addressed the constable. "Are we in perfect agreement?" she asked. "I don't want any problems."

The constable nodded his head. Suddenly, McAdams ran over and barked his orders to the constable. "Get them out of here immediately. I am in charge here not them."

Without any hesitation, Megan moved to McAdams, thrust her finger in his face and shouted, "Listen up you sack of shit, you have no standing here until after the auction. Now get your ass out of here. We have business to conduct."

"I have every right to be here. I own this company."

Megan looked at the constable and pointed to the door. "Get him out of here!"

Before the constable could direct McAdams out of the office, the door to the office opened and in walked Phil Elmore with Woody Coppell in tow. "I will like owning this place. Woody, get me the latest financials. I want to see just how badly Ferrell there has run the place into the dust since I last looked at the books."

Before Woody could make a step, Peter moved to block his forward progress. "We just told the constable to show McAdams to the door, and you two assholes can follow. Until the auction is over, you have no right to be here, except as a bidder out on the yard."

"You don't own this company anymore Ferrell, I do," shouted Elmore.

"You don't own anything until after the auction, which by the way hasn't even started."

Elmore stood erect and crossed his arms over his chest. "I'm not moving," he replied.

McAdams stepped forward. "Neither am I."

"Heather, call security," Peter shouted in a jovial tone. "You will be promptly removed from this office by force. We will be more than happy to ensure you earn a few well placed cuts and bruises in the process."

McAdams looked to the constable for support but he saw that an enormous grin occupied the majority of the man's face. It was clear that he thought Peter's last comments were hilarious. Anger boiled over in McAdams but he wisely backed down. He looked at his auctioneer. "Let's get outside and get thing over with," he ordered as he stormed out of the door with Elmore and Coppell in close pursuit.

The clock on the wall indicated that it was already five ten. Megan instructed Peter and Heather to move into the conference room. Once inside, she locked the door and slammed a stack of papers on the table. From outside, they heard the auctioneer begin to recite the instructions for the auction. "We need to make this quick," she told the group.

CHAPTER 22

"I have a quorum of the owners of Transportation Management Services present either in person or through powers of attorney which I hold in my hand."

The meeting of the owners of the company progressed rapidly under the guidance of Megan Cedars and her expert organizational skills. She was a consummate professional and did not waste precious time on pomp and circumstance. It was strictly a business meeting nothing more. Sidebar conversations were not allowed and distractions were not tolerated. Nonetheless, Peter fidgeted throughout the whole meeting. Heather, as recording secretary for the meeting, took copious minutes on her laptop computer as instructed by Megan. It was essential that every aspect of the meeting was conducted above board and that the permanent record of the meeting was complete and accurate.

Within a few minutes, the business of the three owners was complete. Megan directed Heather to call Bill Cobb into the meeting so that he could execute the wishes of the owners. Prior to the meeting, Megan prepared typed motions for the owners to approve. With the votes cast and tallied, she quickly signed all of the required documents to support the next series of actions. She reviewed the minutes and signed them as corporate secretary.

While waiting for Cobb to join the meeting, Peter moved near Megan. Outside, the sounds of the auctioneer could be heard. He recited the description of the rolling stock, the first group of assets to be auctioned. As she hurriedly ran through the work, he whispered into her ear. "Do you have any final report from the investigator?"

"Thanks for reminding me," she replied without breaking stride in her work. "I nearly forgot." She reached into her black leather tote and retrieved a thick bound report. She handed it to Peter. "Here is what happened. Deutsch was working for a second tier bank in Cleveland a couple of years ago. Within a year of his arrival, he sold a loan to Venture Funding without approval from bank management. Exact same thing pattern as here, solid asset value and a minor technical compliance violation. McAdams foreclosed and it got nasty. There was a fight at the auction sale and the owner was killed by one of the security goons hired by Venture Funding. Both the bank and Venture Funding were sued by the family and quietly settled for a large sum. They forced a sealed settlement agreement. Somehow McAdams escaped being named personally in the suit."

"This is incredible," Peter said softly. "These guys are worse than crooks!"

"You were in their sights long before you realized. This has been a set-up from the start. In retrospect, I should have considered the possibility of this earlier. But with time so short, we just started running and never stopped to take inventory."

Peter rapped his fist on the table. "That's why we have been behind the eight ball and couldn't see around it."

"Precisely! They don't want this information publicized. They both barely missed jail time. Once the FBI puts the two incidents together, I believe they will serve time."

"Can we use this?"

"I don't see how. It just proves that they are crooks. Besides, the auction is already started."

The two stopped talking to hear where the auction stood. They realized that the auctioneer was calling for final bids on the rolling stock. Peter stood and started to run toward the door of the room.

"Where are you going?" Megan cried. "We haven't heard from Ivey. There is nothing you can do. Don't make matters worse!"

"Call Ivey and see where they are," Peter ordered. "Now that I know for certain that these guys are crooks, I think I can call their bluff." Without another word, Peter quickly exited the conference as Cobb entered. In his haste to get to the auction, he nearly knocked Cobb to the floor. He ran as fast as he could through the office and stepped onto the porch.

CHAPTER 23

The crowd turned and gasped when Peter appeared outside TMS' offices. His emergence interrupted the auctioneer's delivery causing him to stop in mid-sentence. At the edge of the porch, Peter leaned on the railing and scanned to assembled group. The auctioneer cleared his throat and announced that bidding on the rolling stock was stalled at four million dollars. The crowd turned their attention once again to the activity at the podium. Without hesitation Peter shouted over the heads of the crowd, "Six million dollars!"

The auctioneer said nothing and completely refused to acknowledge Peter's bid. He looked at McAdams for direction. Peter shouted once more, "This is an auction is it not? I bid six million dollars for the rolling stock of Transportation Management Services!"

McAdams and Elmore say nothing. From where he stood, Peter heard Elmore ask McAdams. "What's that bastard think he's doing? The bids are all prearranged. I don't want to get screwed at the eleventh hour."

"I don't know what the kid is doing. He has no money and is just tooling us around. Stick to our agreement."

"I think not. I know a weasel when I smell one. You have conspired with Ferrell to bid up my price. I should have known better than to trust you," he screamed as he moved a few feet from McAdams.

"Keep your shirt on Phil," McAdams insisted as he walked close to his partner. "I'm not working with Ferrell. Whatever he is doing, he is doing it on his own. I don't want this auction fractured."

"Then get off your ass and take action to put a stop to his shenanigans," Elmore instructed. "Tell you auctioneer to ignore his bid."

McAdams called out to the auctioneer. "That man's bid is not acceptable. He has no cash and can't fund. I won't accept any bid from Ferrell."

The auctioneer looked sternly at McAdams and replied, "Mr. McAdams you made no restrictions regarding the acceptability of the bidders today. All bidders can qualify after the sale. If they can't fund, then the second highest bidder will be allowed to buy the assets. As a registered auctioneer in Texas, I must comply with the requirements of the law. I can make exceptions but only if I outline them in my instructions to the bidder pool prior to the commencement of this auction. Once the auction starts, I am prohibited by law from changing the rules."

Total frustration was etched across McAdams' face. He walked to the podium, covered the microphone with his hand and addressed the auctioneer. "Give me a minute."

The auctioneer thought for a few seconds then replied to McAdams' plea for a pause in the auction. "You have one minute. Then I will restart the auction. One minute, that's all Mr. McAdams."

McAdams jumped from the podium and walked briskly across the yard to the porch where Peter stood. "What are you doing?" he asked. "You have no business being here."

"I have every right to be here. It is still my company."

"What do you want?" he demanded. "I don't have time to play your game. I have a great deal at stake here and I will not allow you to fuck it up!"

"I'm buying my company," Peter responded calmly. "It is an auction after all."

McAdams took a deep breath and reined his temper. "You don't have funding to pull this off," McAdams asserted growing angrier by the moment. "If you want money, we can talk after the auction. Maybe I was hasty in my treatment of you back in Chicago. But now is not the time to make a stand."

"Union Bank is backing me," Peter reported. "I have all of the money I need to buy out your loan."

"Liar!"

"Union Bank is quite upset with that little stunt you and Deutsch pulled. If you don't believe me call Deutsch!"

The conversation was interrupted when the auctioneer called for a resumption of bidding. Immediately, McAdams stormed off and returned to his place next to Elmore. "Get on with the auction."

"What's his game?" Elmore asked his bewildered partner. "What is our next move?"

"I don't know but don't let him screw this deal up. Out bid him!" McAdams demanded. "I want this put to bed immediately."

Elmore raised his hand and shouted, "Seven million dollars."

Everyone in attendance turned and looked directly at Peter. He said nothing further and stood quietly on the porch. McAdams and Elmore looked at one another but said nothing.

With no further bids for the rolling stock, the auctioneer pounded his gavel on the makeshift table and declared the outcome of the first bid to the crowd. "Sold for seven million dollars to Dallas Metro Trucking and Mr. Phil Elmore!"

The auctioneer and his staff took a few minutes to complete and verify the required paperwork. Once it was completed, the auctioneer addressed the group. "The next item up for sale is the real estate of Transportation Management Services." The description of the property took a full five minutes to read. During the reading of the property descriptions, Peter stuck his head inside the door to the office and saw Heather sitting at her desk. "Anything yet?" he asked. "This is moving fast."

Heather shook her head from side to side and responded to Peter's inquiry. "The phone has been silent."

Peter returned to the railing just as the auctioneer started with the sale of the real estate. "Let's open bidding on the real estate at two million dollars. Do I have two million dollars?" he shouted.

The crowd was silent. McAdams and Elmore looked at Peter, but Peter remained silent. "I told you he was only messing with us," McAdams told Elmore. "Make your bid."

Elmore raised his arm and the auctioneer immediately recognized his bid. "I have a bid of two million dollars from Dallas Metro Trucking. Are there any other bids?" the auctioneer called out. The crowd looked for other raised hands within the group, but saw none.

There did not appear to be any other bidders. The auctioneer repeated the bid then raised his gavel signifying that the bidding on the real estate would be closed shortly. "Going once, going twice…"

"Four million dollars," shouted Peter from the porch.

"I have four million dollars from Mr. Peter Ferrell," the auctioneer announced. He looked at McAdams and Elmore for a higher bid.

Peter observed that the two men were once again arguing. Then Elmore raised his arm and shouted, "Four and a half million dollars."

Without a second's delay Peter upped the bid. "Four million, seven hundred and fifty thousand dollars!" The crowd gasped at Peter's bid.

Elmore and McAdams now argued so loudly that their banter could be heard throughout the terminal. "Listen McAdams, I don't need the real estate. I don't know why Ferrell is even bidding. He has lost the rolling stock."

"There are other reasons that you must bid as we agreed. You don't understand all of the implications and I don't have time to explain everything to you now. We need to close the bids out cleanly. I don't want questions afterwards. Dammit man, follow through with your commitment," McAdams shouted.

Clearly frustrated, Elmore once again raised his arm signaling his intention to bid. The auctioneer pointed at Elmore with the gavel. "What do you bid Mr. Elmore?"

"Five million dollars."

Peter said nothing. The total of the bids stood at twelve million dollars. In order to pay the loan off in full, bids needed to total twenty-two million dollars. Peter wasn't even close at this point. A huge multimillion-dollar gap remained to be covered before the debt could be extinguished. McAdams stepped to the podium and whispered into the auctioneer's ear. Immediately the auctioneer hammered the gavel on the podium to silence the crowd. He then addressed the crowd with his final instructions. "We are now going to sell the balance of the assets in one final sale."

By this time, Peter paced back and forth on the porch with his head hung low. There was still no word from Ivey. He didn't want to go inside the office to check with Megan because the final sale was starting.

After the auctioneer announced that the remaining assets would be combined in the last lot for sale, McAdams motioned for him to move along quickly. To save time, the auctioneer omitted the reading of the list of remaining assets. He merely stated that all remaining assets covered under the chattel mortgage held by Venture Funding would be sold to the highest bidder.

"Do I have any bids?"

"Eight million dollars," Elmore shouted as McAdams looked at Peter and smiled.

Peter immediately moved the bid to nine million dollars.

Pressed by McAdams, Elmore upped his bid to nine and a half million dollars. Then the auctioneer called for final bids. Neither Elmore nor McAdams said a word. All eyes were on Peter Ferrell standing alone near the door to the office. Once again the auctioneer called for final bids. Quietness settled over the terminal. It was so quiet that a phone ringing deep in the terminal could be heard.

"Going once, going twice," the auctioneer announced as he raised the gavel to finalize the sale. Peter stood motionless. His mind was racing and his heart was ready to burst from his chest. The auctioneer took one last measure of the crowd and cocked his wrist.

Suddenly Peter heard someone tapping on the office window. He turned and saw Megan flashing the thumbs up sign. He spun around and as the gavel fell quickly toward the podium he shouted, "Twelve and a half million dollars." In his peripheral vision Peter recognized two familiar people walking through the main gate to the terminal. It was Stuart and Valerie. They soon joined Peter on the porch and nodded approvingly.

The auctioneer repeated Peter's bid. "I have twelve and a half million dollars. Can I get thirteen million dollars?"

Elmore elbowed his way through the crowd and stood directly in front of the podium. "The kid's too late. I'm the highest bidder. This auction is over!" he screamed.

The auctioneer disagreed and told the crowd that Peter's bid was made in the instant before the gavel struck the podium. The auction was still open. Dejected, Elmore walked away from the podium. He understood that it was useless to argue with a licensed auctioneer. They were in complete control of the bidding process. McAdams, upon seeing Elmore walk away from the auction, ran to his partner. "What are you doing? You need to buy the contracts. That's the crown jewel of this company. Without them we have nothing. Raise the bid!" McAdams demanded. "We have come too far to throw up our hands now. Don't be a fool."

Megan and Heather stepped out of the office and stood next to Peter. They heard the shouting and decided to move outside and see for themselves what was transpiring. Their timing could not have been better. Tempers were at their maximum. Elmore and McAdams were shouting at one another as the crowd parted around them.

With pure anger venting from his eyes, Elmore turned and accused McAdams. "I think you and Ferrell are in this together to screw me. I'm done here. I'm going back to Dallas. If you want the contracts you better outbid him. We can settle up later. That was the plan from the beginning."

McAdams grabbed Elmore and shook him violently. "Who are you working for?" he shouted. "We had a deal!"

"I'm working for myself like always," Elmore laughed as he pushed off from McAdams.

McAdams was furious. "Why are you doing this to me?"

"Because my friend from the start you planned to do it to me first."

Without another word exchanged, Elmore returned to his car. Again McAdams attempted to stop Elmore. "We have to finish the sale!"

The auctioneer is called for final bids. Reluctantly, McAdams turned and called out to the auctioneer. "Thirteen million dollars!"

The gavel slammed down and the operating assets of the company were no more.

CHAPTER 24

Within seconds of the final fall of the gavel, the crowd dispersed. Peter turned and hugged Megan and Valerie. "You did it," he whispered to Megan. "You are unbelievable. Your strategy worked perfectly. Those bastards never had a chance."

"It wasn't my plan that worked. It was excellent execution on your part. I can't believe you pulled it off. McAdams and Elmore are desperately trying to figure out what hit them broadside."

Peter stood proud that they defeated a rather formidable opponent. He looked at Megan. "You didn't think I had it in me did you?"

"Frankly no!" she replied with a smile. "But I love the way you constantly surprise me."

They looked out over the terminal yard and saw McAdams shoving his way through the remaining crowd toward the office. Peter, Megan and Heather turned and walked back inside the office. Following quickly behind them was Marler McAdams along with Stuart and Valerie. With all of the key players gathered in the reception area, Megan invited them to move into the large conference room. She also signaled for the constable to join them. Before he took a single step, McAdams unleashed his wrath. "I want you all out of my office. Get out immediately!" he shouted. He turned to the constable. "I know my rights now! Escort them out immediately."

The group laughed at McAdams' grandstanding. Megan stepped forward. "What exactly do you own Mr. Big Mac?" she asked.

"I bought everything at the auction. So get out!"

Megan cocked her head then raised her right index finger to her right temple. "If I recall from the auction, Dallas Metro Trucking purchased the real estate not you." She turned to the constable and continued. "Did Mr. Elmore leave any instructions with you regarding clearing the property once the auction finished. I believe he is no longer on the premises and therefore unable to issue any fresh instructions."

The constable flashed a broad smile and replied to Megan. "I did not meet with Mr. Elmore today. I have no instructions concerning the property. I was invited here by Mr. McAdams and directed to ensure the auction went off without incident. Since the auction is finished, my job here is done."

"Correct me if I'm wrong, but I believe that under the law even if Mr. Elmore had given instructions, Mr. Ferrell has twenty-four hours to remove our personal possessions from the property after an auction."

"That is correct Ms. Cedars," the constable replied. Without another word, the constable tipped his hat and departed the office.

With the issue of legal standing settled, the group shuffled quietly into the conference room. Once everyone was settled in around the large conference table Megan addressed the group. "Today, we witnessed the end of an era. TMS is no longer an operating company. I am here to report to the owners that all of the assets but one have been dispersed, sold or liquidated."

"This is all a bunch of crap if you ask me," McAdams told the group in a huff. "You got nothing."

"On the contrary, there is one asset left in the company but we will discuss that in a minute," Megan replied with a smile. "In other news, we sold the customer contracts earlier today for twelve million dollars to Martin Ivey at Coastal Truckers. I believe he is presently out in the terminal offering jobs to our former employees. The deal is closed and recorded with all of the filings effective. The money has already been disbursed to the shareholders in accordance to their ownership percentages."

"You can't sell the contracts, I own them," McAdams laughed sarcastically. "What are you trying to pull here? My attorneys are just a phone call away."

"I reviewed your loan documents personally," Megan disclosed to their visitor from Chicago. "And I discovered several serious omissions in the asset schedules supporting the bank's original loan, which Venture Funding now owns."

McAdams set back in his chair and rested his hands on the table. "What are you talking about?" he asked clearly pretending to have no knowledge of the facts.

"It seems the bank liens you purchased were incomplete," Megan stated very succinctly. "You didn't hold all of the collateral you thought."

"Leslie confirmed that the error to which you refer was not material," McAdams confessed. "Those documents were perfect."

"You know Leslie Goodwin my paralegal?" Megan asked McAdams as he squirmed in his chair. "I'm surprised that you would rely upon the opinion of an hourly paralegal to make multimillion dollar decisions. I would have thought that you of all people were smarter than that."

McAdams though about his comments then recanted his earlier claims. "No, I don't know anyone by that name."

Megan looked at Peter and smiled. She then moved close McAdams and shook her finger in his face. "Listen Big Mac, I'm not trying to pull anything, much less anything of yours. Call your big shot lawyer in Chicago. You didn't get the contracts or for that matter the receivables or their proceeds. They were not included in the asset schedules attached to the operative loan documents. Likewise the county filings are incomplete."

McAdams laughed a sinister laugh. "My Chicago lawyer knows about the supposed error. It is merely a technically. I have case law on my side. The intent of your client was to pledge all of the assets, including contracts and receivables."

"Maybe that's the way it works in Illinois, but in Texas, documents rule my friend. Since the loan was renewed twice with the error, you are standing on thin ice. You should have sprung for a competent Texas lawyer to review the documents before you bought the loan."

McAdams groused around in his seat. "I relied on Deutsch."

"That was clearly a mistake on your part," Peter chirped. "I know. He did a substandard job managing my relationship with Union Bank."

McAdams lost his temper and screamed. "I own 49% of this company! And there is over a million dollars in cash in the coffers."

"How do you figure you own 49%?" Megan asked trying her best to hold back a flood of laughter.

"I just bought Ferrell's stock at the auction. Were you not paying attention?"

"You didn't buy any stock. The stock was pledged behind his guarantee and since the proceeds from the auction cleared the debt, the guarantee falls. You and Mr. Elmore have nothing but some trucks and a falling down terminal."

"I own the contracts!"

"No you don't!" Megan shouted.

"I've been duped. I overpaid."

"Duped by whom?" Megan asked. "This was your auction if you remember. You have absolutely no legal standing to refute your own credit bid at your auction."

McAdams immediately countered. "I'll put this company in bankruptcy and get the courts to order the money returned to me."

Megan pushed a razor thin smile to her lips. "How do you plan to accomplish that? You don't own the company and I just told you that all other creditors were paid in full prior to the auction. It takes three creditors to file an involuntary bankruptcy. Since your debt is paid, you are no longer a creditor. And as far as company cash is concerned, all remaining cash balances in the company's accounts were paid out to the three owners just before the auction started."

"I'm owed money on the loan I bought from Union Bank and I will collect all that is due. You are not going to push me around."

"I beg your pardon Marler," Megan said working hard to maintain her professional demeanor. "How do you figure there is a balance remaining on the loan you acquired from Union Bank? Were you not at the auction? The bids at the auction totaled twenty-five million dollars. Your note balance was only twenty-two million dollars. You are not a creditor any longer. Besides, the shell of TMS was placed into bankruptcy only minutes ago and we have no plans to contest the auction."

"What are you babbling about? I have a twenty-two million loan from TMS and Ferrell's guarantee."

"You sold all of the assets of TMS at your auction. The three winning bids paid your loan in full."

McAdams paused, stood and stepped back a few feet. The finality of Megan's remarks hit him hard. In the frenzy of the auction, he failed to keep track of the bidding. With Elmore in his pocket and the auction pre-packaged to come in below the debt, he never considered this possible outcome. It was now clear that Peter and Megan outsmarted him magnificently.

"So if we do the math on the auction proceeds and based on your bid for the remaining assets after the rolling stock and real estate, you owe TMS three million dollars," Megan detailed. "Please call your lawyer and have him wire the funds to Houston immediately. I don't want to speak for the owners, but I don't believe they are willing to accept a check from you."

"Are you insane?" McAdams screamed. "My bid was a creditor bid. There is no cash payment required."

"Your creditor bid in Texas is the same as cash if the total of the bids exceed the balance due on the underlying loan. The assets sold for three million dollars in excess of the debt."

"I will see you in court and get the creditor bid overturned."

"You can't overturn a creditor bid." Megan announced that based upon the bid at the foreclosure, there is no deficiency and all actions of the TMS owners cannot be reversed. "In Texas foreclosure sales are final and not subject to appeal. I have requested an independent trustee in the bankruptcy to collect all sums due. Since the three folks in this room own the company, you owe them three million dollars."

"I'll never pay. I'll sue your client and bring you up on ethics charges before the Texas Bar."

"Go ahead and start legal action against the Ferrell family. We demand our day in court, especially since you cleverly deprived us of our hearing earlier today. I know all about Cleveland and I will get the settlement unsealed. I know about your side deal with Elmore and I know that you paid my paralegal to conspire against my client. If you bring legal action, I am convinced that you and your co-conspirator Jeff Deutsch will then get to see the inside of our prisons here in Texas. Your days profiting from the misery of others are over. If you don't mind, my suggestion is that you spare yourself the agony of a trial and simply wire transfer three million dollars from your Chicago bank immediately."

"You don't scare me," McAdams barked. "I eat folks like you for lunch every day."

Peter piped up from across the table. "After today Mac, all you will be eating is that high priced whore of yours in Chicago."

Megan once again addressed their guest. "I can assure you Mr. McAdams I am not trying to scare you. Fear is your game, not mine. I'm a simple corporate lawyer that kicked your sorry ass today."

"I still won't pay."

"Somehow I knew that would be your position and that's why I petitioned for an independent trustee to complete the liquidation of the company. Trust me you will pay him. If you don't, the funds will be withheld from the other proceeds of the sale."

McAdams turned red as a beet and stormed out of the conference room. Without a word to anyone in the office, he exited the office slamming the door with a crash after he passed. Peter and Megan stepped out on the porch and saw the workers gathering around Martin Ivey who arrived earlier. He told the TMS staff that he wanted them to continue to work at his terminal which would be reopened shortly.

Marler McAdams stood alone at the bottom of the steps mumbling as he reviewed his notes. As Peter and Megan walked past their nemesis to depart the terminal for the last time, McAdams turned to the couple and screamed, "What do you expect me to do?"

Peter paused, smiled then looked him squarely in the eyes and casually remarked, "Why Marler McAdams, I expect you to do nothing."

Megan grabbed Peter's arm, spun him around and flashed a deep smile. "Let's go to Vegas!"

ABOUT THE AUTHOR

Jim Ardoin lives in the Intermountain West and is the author of the following books:

The Greedhawkers

Borrowed Money

Misdirection

At the Bottom of the Deep Ravine

All of these books are available at www.amazon.com. If you would like to contact Jim, please visit his website www.jimardoin.com.

Made in the USA